NIKOLAI

His Reluctant Submissive - Book 2

JESSIE JONES

Published by Blushing Books
An Imprint of
ABCD Graphics and Design, Inc.
A Virginia Corporation
977 Seminole Trail #233
Charlottesville, VA 22901

Jessie Jones
Nikolai

Print ISBN: 978-1-63954-003-7
v1

Chapter 1

"**Y**ou're late, Piper!" yelled the short, pudgy man in a navy-blue suit as he stood at the bar tapping his watch. "You know I don't like it when my girls are late."

"I know, Al, so get off my back. I'm not in the mood today," the blonde shouted back, hurriedly making her way past the bar. "I told you a month ago that I might be late on Fridays due to med school."

Stepping in front of Piper, Al shot out a hand and gripped her upper arm. "Give me one good reason why I shouldn't fire your pretty ass, sweetheart."

"Go ahead and fire me!" she shot back hotly, her clear blue eyes shooting daggers at him. She hated the sleazy bastard and couldn't wait to be done with the club scene. "Next month, I'm out of this hell hole anyway. Now take your hands off me! I've got to change so I can start my shift."

"We have a full club this evening, Williamson. There are even a couple of guys who specifically requested to see you in the VIP lounge."

1

"Great," she said sarcastically, rolling her eyes. "They're probably real perverts then."

"Well, whatever they are, you know I get a cut of the VIP profit, kid. The foreign guy assured me that they just want to watch you dance. They are paying triple the fee, so there was no turning it down. Brian will be outside the room the whole time if things should go south. There is no way I'd let my number one money maker get hurt."

"You're such a repulsive pig," Piper replied tightly in disgust as she jerked her arm from the man's grip. As she walked past the club owner and toward the dressing room, she felt unshed tears burning her eyes as she flipped the man off before disappearing behind the purple curtain. Once on the other side of the thick, linen door, Piper Williamson closed her eyes a moment and took a deep, cleansing breath. *One more month, and you will never have to degrade yourself for money again,* she told herself. Opening her eyes, she walked to her make-up table and dropped her heavy backpack beside the chair. Plopping down, the blonde stuck out her tongue as she looked at herself in the mirror. She couldn't believe how tired she looked today. Between her job at the club, the hospital, and her first year of medical school, she was swamped. Thankfully, she had the weekend off and hopefully could catch up on some much-needed rest and relaxation.

Undoing the clip in her thick, curly hair, she watched it fall midway down her back. Eyes the color of the deepest ocean stared back as she thought about the events of today. Not only had she been late for class this morning, but one of the senior doctors had recognized her from the club. He, of course, had made a pass at her and when she told him to go to hell, he failed her skills assessment. Although she had reported the incident to the ethics supervisor, she knew nothing would be done. She had gone to great lengths to hide her identity at the club but sometimes the wigs she wore just didn't work. Piper was not proud to be dancing for money, but men liked the way she looked. The problem was they never took time to look beyond the physical. In the short twenty-three years of her existence, she had yet to meet a man who wasn't a complete and utter asshole. Every man she had encountered throughout her life had wanted something from her and when she wouldn't give it to them, they would simply try to take it. Piper, however, had learned several tricks along the way and knew how to safeguard not only her body, but her mind and heart.

With another loud sigh, she began prepping for an evening of work. She hated working as a dancer in the strip club but at this point in life, she really needed the money. Not only was medical school ridiculously expensive, but she had no one else to rely on financially. Every penny she made, she saved toward school and basic bills. She almost had enough to quit the club and had just started a job at the hospital as a lab tech. She might dress provocatively at the club, but she never removed her clothing during a performance. Due to her choice of temporary professions, men frequently offered her a relationship as well as wealth beyond her wildest dreams. She had lost count of the numbers of offers she had received from them, but there was no way in hell Piper was going to acquire anything on her back. Because of the way men treated her, Piper had zero respect for them and that unfortunately resulted in her having an overall low opinion of the opposite sex. That low opinion was not a recent one but had started with a man named Maury Brennan.

Thinking of her dead stepfather had the tall blonde's skin crawling in absolute disgust. Growing up with the bastard in east Texas, had been extremely scary and a literal hell on earth. Not only had she grown up in abject poverty and squalor, but Maury had been physically and mentally abusive to all those living in the household. His "love" had unfortunately killed her mother, Lynn, when Piper was seven. With

JESSIE JONES

her mother dead and her stepfather locked up for murder, she had immediately been sent to foster care and spent the next eleven years in the system, bouncing from home to home. He had attempted to reach out to her when she turned eighteen, but she had shut that down quickly. Maury had passed away sick and lonely, in a state prison, just a couple of years ago and Piper was glad to see him go. The only thing he had left that was of any value was a biological daughter named Andy Brennan, who was the only family Piper had. Although they were not biologically related, the two of them had grown up in the trenches. Unfortunately for Andy, her life had been even worse than her own.

Piper had been four years of age when eleven-year-old Andy had come into her life. She was Maury's only child and moved in with them when he had married her mother. The two were close as children and her stepsister had gone to great lengths to protect her from Maury's drunken, physical abuse. Unfortunately for Piper, Andy had been forced to live with her real mother when Maury had killed Lynn. At that point, the two girls lost contact and had only been able to reconnect when she turned eighteen and left foster care. Andy found her about a month after that and invited her to move to Las Vegas so the younger woman could start over and enroll in college. Now the two shared a condo together and Piper had just graduated with a bachelor's in premed from UNLV and was starting her first year of med school. Although Andy would never take it, Piper had every intention of repaying her for all the kindness and assistance she had given her the last five years. They were both poor economically but rich with their love for one another.

Sitting down in the makeup chair, she pulled on her black, spiky boots before applying her make-up and short, brown wig. Looking at herself in the mirror again, Piper thought about her personal life. She hated the overwhelming loneliness she felt sometimes. If only she could be as beautiful and outgoing as Andy. Yeah, men found her physically attractive, but she had a hard time seeing what they saw. Piper didn't consider herself difficult to get along with per se, but she trusted no one and felt as though she had too much emotional baggage for any man to love. Deep down, she was a sucker for romance and had been involved with a handful of men, but each of those relationships had ended horribly. One had been married, one had tried to beat her up, and the others were total failures. There had been one decent guy in the sea of losers, but she had ruined it by unintentionally sabotaging the relationship. She was just someone who was better off being alone. Although she desperately wanted a man who would talk and cuddle and explore her body sexually, she didn't know if she would ever find him.

Putting the final touches on her make-up, Piper walked over to her closet and pulled out a black two-piece outfit that consisted of booty shorts and a black, vest style top. Sliding them on, she again admired her appearance in the mirror. She looked the part of an exotic dancer and could commit to the role; however, it was just that, an act. She often got put in the VIP lounge because of her physical appearance. They frequently requested sexual favors, but Piper was simply not interested. Not once had a man ever treated her like a human being. No one outside of Andy knew the intimate details of her life but then again, no one had asked. Maybe men only wanted her sexually because they innately knew that she was an emotional mess. Piper had a bad habit of ending relationships with men before they even began. If she did that, then she didn't have to worry about getting hurt.

Seeing the large security guard step into the room, had her sighing loudly and rolling her neck. She then followed Brian through the club and up to the VIP area. When she exited the elevator, Piper was surprised to see two giant men staring openly at her. They said something in a foreign language before they opened the curtain and allowed her to step in. She motioned with her hand for Brian to follow but was thrown off when the two men blocked his movements with their massive bodies.

"Nyet. Stays here," the taller man said with a sneer.

"No!" Piper returned forcibly. "Either Brian goes in with me or I walk."

The man's response was to roughly push her through the linen door. She heard Brian shouting at the two men before everything went eerily quiet. Hearing someone clear his throat, she turned around and focused on the two men sitting on the leather, camel brown sofa. The shorter man had dark blond hair that was graying on the sides and blue eyes. There was something cold and indifferent about the way he was looking at her. The taller man with black hair was downright scary. She hated the way his green eyes moved over her body like a vulture eyeing its next meal.

"So, you're the entertainment?" the shorter man asked from where he stood. "We have been waiting for you. My name is Paul Morrison, and this is my friend Grecoff Chechen. Please have a seat."

"Like I told your guards, I'm not going anywhere unless Brian is allowed in," Piper replied sternly, refusing to move. Why did she have a sense of dread and unease building in her stomach?

"We have no intention of hurting you so there is no reason why he would need to stay. We actually don't even need to be entertained, but we would like to talk to Piper Williamson."

"How the hell do you..." she began in utter shock but stopped herself before confirming her identity. "I'm sorry, but I don't know who this Piper person is. Why don't I just get you guys a drink?"

"Come closer, Piper," Paul said, motioning her toward

them with his hand. "We don't want to force you, but we will. We only want to ask you some questions."

She reluctantly walked toward the men but refused to sit as she watched the two men lean forward on the sofa. "What is all of this about? Who are you?"

"We already told you who we are, now we just need a little information about you," Paul replied, pulling out a cigarette to smoke. "Think you can help us?"

Letting out a shaky sigh, Piper wanted to run. However, something told her that she was not dealing with average, ordinary men. These men, by the cut of their clothes, clearly had money and that often meant that they had access to unlimited power. There was also something about their demeanor that told her these men were tied to some type of international crime ring. Maybe if she just did as they asked, they would leave. "I don't know." she heard herself say in a calm voice. "What are you wanting to know exactly?"

"First, let's talk about where you're from and who your parents are," Paul said as he leaned back on the sofa and crossed his legs.

She was surprised by the first question that came out of the smaller man's mouth. Why the hell would they need to know that? Was she in some sort of trouble? Piper knew little about her family history because her mother had been a drug addict before being murdered. "I'm originally from Texas and my mom's name was Lynn Williamson. I don't know who my father was. I don't even know if my mom did."

"How old were you when Lynn died?" he asked, watching her intently.

"I was seven when she was murdered," Piper replied, wringing her hands together nervously. She hated the way the two men, especially the dark-haired one, looked at her.

"Did she ever tell you about her parents?"

"Mom never really talked about her family. I think I might

have met my grandfather once, but he was dying of cancer in the hospital."

"Do you remember his name or anything about him?"

"No. We saw him in the hospital and were there about an hour. He seemed kind and talked to me. He told me I looked exactly like his dead wife. Other than that, I don't remember what he said to me."

"Did your mother have any other children?"

"She told me once that I have a half-brother who is older than I am, but I never met the guy. I don't know his name or even if he's alive." Piper shrugged as she watched the two men look at each other and say something in a foreign language. She, however, was growing increasingly agitated with their line of questioning. "Look, I don't know why you are asking these kinds of questions, but I'm not going to answer anything further unless you tell me why you need the information."

Paul did not appreciate the attitude he heard in the woman's voice. If he could, he would kill the bitch right where she stood, but unfortunately, he couldn't. Little did the blonde know, but he was the half-brother she mentioned and was asking the questions because Piper was the key to his inheriting millions of dollars. The only problem was he had no idea where the money was, exactly, but he did know that he had to have Piper alive to get it. Looking at the man who sat beside him, Paul said, "I have no doubts it's her, Grecoff. Do you think she's lying?"

"No, I don't, but I think we need to check out her apartment just in case," Grecoff replied.

"I agree. I doubt she has anything, though. In her records, it says she was placed in foster care when she was seven. There was no way she would have remembered anything specific about inheriting money, but we need to be sure. I say we take a trip to Texas and see what we can find out relating to the old man's will and where the money might be."

"Are we taking this little beauty with us?" Grecoff asked, rubbing his hands together eagerly. The woman was gorgeous and just his type.

"No. Somehow, I don't think she would go quietly, and that's attention we don't need. She's not going anywhere, and the Volkovs have no idea that we're here. We'll just come back and get her when we need to. We have too much at stake right now and it's going to be important to follow the plan, especially if we want to destroy Aleksandr and Nikolai."

"Fucking Volkovs!" Grecoff growled as he spat on the floor. "I'll be glad when both of those fuckers are dead and rotting in the ground."

Piper watched the interaction between the two men and knew they were talking about her although she didn't understand their words. When she cleared her throat uncomfortably, both men looked at her. "If you guys don't have any more questions, I'm going to leave."

"We're done with our questions, but I don't think I'm done with you." The Russian bratva leader smiled as he stood up and walked toward her.

"Yeah, well, I am," Piper countered nervously, but as she turned to leave, Grecoff grabbed her arm and roughly jerked her around. As his hands slid down her body, Piper screamed, "Get your damn hands off me!" To prove her point, she stomped on Grecoff's foot and kneed him in the crotch.

The dark-haired man yelled out before the back of his hand came down painfully across Piper's face. Grabbing his throbbing member through his suit, Grecoff watched in shock and dismay as she looked up at him with eyes full of rage and fury. To try to break her, he slapped her face again, but she did not cower. Before he could hit her a third time, Grecoff felt Paul grab his arm and hold it. In his ear, he heard the man snarl, "We don't need this kind of attention right now! Be patient, my friend. When we get back to Vegas, you can do whatever you want with her. By then, the Volkovs will be dead and the underworld will be ours."

Grecoff grabbed the front of Piper's dress and pulled her toward him. "You're lucky my friend is here, little one, because I would fuck you where you stand and then slit that lovely, delicate neck." He watched her gasp in fear and then felt her body begin to uncontrollably shake. "I knew there was a submissive under that tough exterior. I look forward to breaking your spirit the next time we meet." He then slammed his mouth down on hers as she struggled and pushed violently against his chest. He cried out and dropped her on the floor when she bit his bottom lip and scratched his face. Feeling the blood, he watched her quickly jump to her feet and head toward the exit. Yelling out an order in Russian, the doors opened, and Piper left.

"That one is a real wildcat. I think I'll take her home with me."

"Do whatever you want with her. I only care about the money," Paul countered as the guards closed the gap between them.

"Just got a call," a guard said as he looked at Grecoff. "Viktor and Kira are dead. The police are picking up Volkov as we speak."

Both men burst out laughing. "And so it begins, my friend," Grecoff said with a smile as he put his arm around Paul. "Let's celebrate our victory with a drink. Feels good to have the world at your fingertips, da?"

"You don't know how good," Paul responded as they stood to leave.

Chapter 2

He groaned in pleasure as the brunette pleased him orally. The woman's arms were handcuffed to two of the four bedposts and she wriggled in pleasure as the vibrating toy brought her closer to her own climax. With one final push of his hips, Nikolai felt the orgasm tear through his body. His head fell back in satisfaction as he pulled out of the woman's mouth only to stroke the rest of his essence onto her large, plus size breasts. His muscular, bronze, tattooed body jerked, and his breathing was quick and shallow until the wave of intensity began to subside. When all the tension had left his muscles, Nikolai bent down and kissed the woman on the mouth softly before he removed the handcuffs from her wrists and the toy from between her legs. Sitting down on the side of the bed, he felt the woman crawl up behind him and wrap her arms around his thick, corded neck. She placed kisses on his shoulders and back as she rubbed her breasts against his warm skin.

"What's wrong with you tonight, Sir? Did I not please you?" Katja purred as she kissed his cleanly shaven, masculine jaw. Nikolai did not seem like himself this evening and appeared bothered. "You always lie with me after sex. Did I do something to offend you?"

"You did exactly what I asked you to do, Katja." Nikolai smiled, looking at his tempting submissive. "I just have a lot on my mind this evening. None of which concerns you."

"I hate to see you worried. Is there anything else I can do for you?"

"If only it was that simple, sweetheart," Nikolai said before kissing her softly on the cheek. "Now if you'll excuse me, I have a meeting with Artem in his downtown office that I am late for."

"May I stay here in your bed until morning, Sir?" Katja asked, watching her dominant lover get out of the bed.

"No. You will return to your home and wait for me. Understand?"

"Of course," the woman replied, bowing her head submissively before she climbed out of the bed to begin putting on her clothes. As she dressed, her green eyes watched thirty-year-old Nikolai Volkov doing the same. Her eyes scanned his six feet six, muscular physique that included broad, tattooed shoulders that narrowed to a well-defined stomach. When he turned a moment, the breath caught in her throat as his enormous, soft cock lay between two powerful, athletic thighs that rounded to an ass that was tight, taut, and toned. Her gaze then traveled back up his body to his striking, handsome face. Black, short hair cut in a mohawk fade framed a bronzed, clean-shaven face with a Nordic style nose and full, pink lips. As beautiful as Nikolai's face was, nothing compared to his deep-set grey eyes that changed color slightly with his mood. The man was walking human perfection and was just as attractive internally as he was externally.

With a sigh, she felt her clit twitch between her legs as Nikolai winked at her before he walked into the bathroom to clean up. Katja adored the Russian bratva leader and had been one of his submissives for the last two years. The feelings she felt for him, however, were not reciprocated. She knew her dominant lover cared about her, but he had never professed his love for her, or any woman for that matter. Nikolai, along with his brother Aleksandr, were worth billions and were currently being sought by the mafia council to control the entire underworld. How she wished that he would make her his exclusive submissive but knew he never would. Katja would take what she could get, though. He was a compassionate, giving, honest lover and she was his favorite submissive, even if only for the time being.

When Nikolai walked back into the bedroom of his home, he was dressed in a pair of jeans and a long-sleeved, cream-colored sweater that molded to his muscles. After grabbing his black Bvlgari watch and his cellphone, Nikolai walked past Katja without saying a word and exited the bedroom. Making his way down the elaborate staircase, his mind immediately went to the business. Before leaving his house, a mountain of muscle quickly approached him and fell into lock step. "Have the car brought around, Mikhas. Artem sent me a text and has changed the plan. We are meeting at his place."

Talking into his earpiece, the guard disappeared as Nikolai grabbed his coat and headed out into the frigid air. Climbing into the white SUV, Nikolai kicked back in his seat and closed his eyes. Damn, he was tired but there was no time to rest, especially with their enemies trying to take him and his older brother Aleksandr down. Not only was a man he considered a father brutally murdered, but his brother was wrongly accused of the crime. The knife that had killed Viktor Sergei was found in Aleksandr's NYC suite with his brother's fingerprints on it. However, at the time his brother had supposedly been killing Viktor, he was at a sex club with a woman who was unknowingly a prosecuting attorney and his saving grace. Due to the woman's involvement with Aleksandr, their enemies had tried to kill her, but his brother had anticipated it and foiled the whole thing. Thankfully, Aleksandr was now safe in their homeland and had brought the female attorney, Sophia Rousseau, with him. His brother saving Sophia, had complicated matters greatly but also uncovered a divisive plan to take Nikolai's family down.

Thinking of that plan had his thoughts flashing momentarily to his past. Viktor Sergei had taken him and Aleksandr into his home to raise when their parents were brutally murdered. Nikolai had been three and Aleksandr eleven. His father and Viktor had not only been best friends, but they had led the largest and second largest bratvas respectfully. The individuals who killed Nikolai's parents had also wanted the Volkov siblings dead, so Viktor hid them underground while he sought revenge for the death of his friend. When Aleksandr had been old enough to ascend to the role of bratva leader, Viktor had ensured that his older brother had taken what rightfully belonged to him. Aleksandr and Viktor, along with Nikolai, had financially grown the bratvas and brought much needed reform to the underworld until Paul Morrison had come into the picture. Due to Viktor's declining health and hold over his bratva, Morrison knew that Nikolai and Aleksandr were the only two people standing between him and Viktor's fortune. Because Morrison couldn't destroy the Volkovs on his own, he had enlisted the help of Oleg and Grecoff Chechen. The father and son duo had long been a pain in their asses and hated the Volkov brothers with a passion. The three men wanted nothing more than to annihilate them but there was no way in hell that was ever going to happen.

Feeling his phone vibrate, Nikolai glanced down and read another text message from Artem. Artem Smirnov was the brothers' trusted attorney and one of Nikolai's best friends. He was on his way to see the man because Aleksandr had chosen

Nikolai to take over Viktor's multi-million-dollar business and the bratva itself. They needed to review his assets and decide what would stay and what would go. Plus, there was the little matter of Paul Morrison going to America to find a young woman who was the key to him and the Chechens acquiring half a billion dollars. Apparently, this woman had no idea that she was Paul's half-sister and had no knowledge of the money she was set to inherit. Paul and the Chechens were using this money to recruit men to help them take down Nikolai and his brother. Aleksandr, who had his own shit to deal with, was entrusting Nikolai to go to the States to get this woman before Paul did. Nikolai just needed a few more details to finalize the plan. There was no way in hell that he would ever let Aleksandr down. The two were thick as thieves and he loved him more than anyone else in the world. The fact that the older Volkov was trusting Nikolai to handle something so important, meant everything to him. For so long, Aleksandr had tried to protect Nikolai from bratva life but he refused to let everything fall on his brother's shoulders. He was finally taking his position as Aleksandr's right-hand man and that is exactly where he wanted to be.

When the car came to a stop at Artem's home, Nikolai climbed out of the SUV and quickly headed inside. He was immediately met on the inside by a pretty, young maid who was staring at him lustfully. A handsome smile touched Nikolai's mouth as he removed his coat. "Hello, Sabina. How are you this evening?"

"I'm wonderful, Mr. Volkov," the brunette replied with a wide smile, taking his coat. "If you don't mind me saying, you look very handsome."

"So do you, sweetheart." Nikolai winked with a chuckle as the woman blushed and melted at his words. He knew he was an attractive man but even Nikolai didn't understand exactly what drew women to him. Sometimes he was thankful for his ease with women and other times, it was a huge pain in his ass. Reaching out to brush Sabina's cheek with his fingers, Nikolai asked, "Can you tell me where Artem is?"

"Just follow me, sir."

Nikolai followed the woman and hid his laughter when she glanced back adoringly at him and batted her eyes. When they reached Artem's office, his friend was on the phone. Mouthing 'thank you' to the woman, he closed the door to the room and walked over to the bar. Pouring himself a drink, he took a seat. Just as he took the first sip, he watched Artem hang up the phone. Seeing the look on his friend's face, Nikolai asked, "Is everything all right?"

"Yeah, it will be," Artem replied as he approached Nikolai and poured himself a drink. "Just working on a case that involves Igor Oleksiy. That asshole needs to investigate the people his son hires a little more. I can't use someone as a credible witness if they are involved in criminal activities. Anyway, enough about work. I hope you're hungry, friend. My staff is preparing dinner as we speak."

"You know I'm always up for a good meal." Nikolai smiled, thinking of one of his favorite pastimes. "I'm sorry I'm late, but I needed to release some tension first."

Artem chuckled as he motioned for Nikolai to follow him to a nearby sofa. "I figured as much. Aleksandr told me you released quite a bit of tension in New York at Andrei's club. I hear our friend may be coming home once you and Aleksandr take over the bratva council."

"Zan doesn't want control of the council and has made that fact known to all parties involved," Nikolai scoffed, thinking of his brother. "However, we both know he'll take it."

"He will as long as you're by his side, Nik," Artem replied, relaxing back on the couch. "Have you given it any thought?"

"I have, and there is no way in hell I would leave my brother to battle the wolves alone. I don't want it any more than he does, but I want what's best for our bratva," Nikolai stated as he too relaxed back on the sofa and crossed his legs. "Before we get down to business, are you looking forward to Club Carnage tonight? I hope you intend on engaging in debauchery with the rest of us. Zan told me that you are no longer seeing Nina. What happened? I thought she might be the one to finally lock you down."

"Yeah, I thought so too, but she couldn't keep her legs together," Artem said in disgust as he rolled his blue eyes. "With her now out of the picture, I plan on engaging in all sorts of activities tonight. Nina never liked being handcuffed or spanked, so those two things are high on my list. I will just have to get to the submissive beauties before you do. Once they see your pretty face, it's all over for the rest of us."

"I can't help it if women like me better than you." Nikolai grinned impishly. "I've told you several times that I am always here to offer pointers should you need them."

"Fuck you!" Artem laughed loudly. "I do fine on my own. I haven't had a submissive complain about my abilities yet. Think Alek will participate tonight?"

"No," the younger Volkov replied, shaking his head in denial. Nikolai had just met the attractive attorney today and Aleksandr couldn't keep his hands off her. His brother had only known the woman a few days and was already acting like a love-sick fool. "I have no doubt he will dominate Sophia, but I think Zan might be done with other women. Did you see the way he treated her today? I've never seen him react that way to a woman. I think I may need to do a little research on Ms. Rousseau."

"Already have, Nik, and she's a brilliant young lady," Artem responded, thinking of Aleksandr and the attractive redhead. "However, you're welcome to look at the file for your-self. She is a mouthy little thing, but there is something about Sophia I like. I actually think she's perfect for Alek."

"Yeah, well, we'll see about that," Nikolai said, rolling his eyes before he noticed a file folder on the coffee table. Picking it up, he asked, "Is this the paperwork on Viktor's assets?"

"Da. Look it over and tell me what you think. I'll see if Olga can bring us in some food."

Nikolai sat there for a few minutes flipping through the papers as Artem had staff bring in dinner. Viktor had at one time been worth an estimated eight billion dollars, but over the past two to three years, he had lost a large portion of that due to cleaning up Paul's poor investments and paying off his daughter Kira's debts. At this time, the total of his assets was a little over three-hundred-million and Nikolai wanted to see that the money was put in an account for Viktor's wife, Anya, to live out her life comfortably. There were also several properties around the world that needed to be sold, but there was only one that Nikolai and Aleksandr would want. He, again, would let Anya decide which ones she wanted and which ones went. After all, the woman was like a mother to the brothers, and it was up to the Volkov boys to ensure she had everything she could want or need. As for leadership of Viktor's bratva, Aleksandr and Nikolai had already addressed that. All the men under Viktor's leadership had assured the brothers that they would have their complete loyalty and full support.

Smelling the authentic Russian beef stroganoff and pirozhki rolls, had Nikolai's stomach growling. Setting the file down, he watched Artem fill a plate. "I didn't realize how much of Viktor's money Paul and Kira had pissed away."

"No one did. Viktor never talked about his finances to anyone," Artem replied, handing Nikolai the plate and glass of wine. "Even Aleksandr was shocked at how much money had been mishandled over the past few years. I hate to say this, but Kira couldn't have been that clueless regarding her husband, Nik. Do you think she was somehow involved in Viktor's death?"

"No, I don't. She loved her father, but she also had blind love for Paul," Nikolai said, taking a bite of the delicious food. "There is no way she would have hurt Anya like that."

"I hope you're right. As far as Viktor's assets, what do you want to do?"

"It all goes into an account for Anya. She will only be able to withdraw large amounts of money with a verbal okay from myself or Aleksandr. As for the properties, we 'll see what she wants and sell the rest. The only property Zan or I want is the small house in Norway."

"Why do you keep that place? I mean, it's beautiful up there but you both could buy the whole damn island if you wanted to," Artem asked with a chuckle. He had been to the small home before with Nikolai and Aleksandr and didn't understand why they loved it so much. The house itself was above the Artic Circle and located on a tiny archipelago. He wasn't even sure how often they got to visit.

"It's sentimental." Nikolai shrugged, wiping his mouth. "Viktor took Zan and me fishing there as boys. Apparently, he and our father used the island as their own personal getaway. We just have some great memories there. It was nice to be a normal kid, doing normal things."

"Well, it was beautiful but a little too far out there for me. I prefer the city." Artem grinned. "You and Aleksandr have the same thoughts regarding Viktor's assets, but he wanted you to make the final decision. How do you plan on handling the transition of power between bratvas?"

"Already taken care of. We met with Viktor's Elite Seven about a week ago. They assured us it would be a smooth conversion. As you know, we have been working with them for a while, so the change was already anticipated. We threw in a large monetary installment to each man who stayed committed to the bratva. We also gave those who wanted out a chance for a clean break. No one chose to leave, thankfully,"

Nikolai replied, putting his plate down a moment to take a drink of wine. "What about this woman Paul and Grecoff are after? What information do we have on her?"

"Ah, yes. Piper Williamson." Artem smiled, thinking of the blonde fondly. As he walked over to get her file, he said, "You might actually like helping this one, Nik. This is one woman I hope comes home with you."

Setting his glass down, Nikolai took the file from Artem. Opening it, he was unprepared for the shock he felt to his system. The breath caught in his throat as he stared at the headshot picture. The woman had a contoured nose and full, cupid bow lips that were a beautiful shade of blush. Nikolai even loved the small mole he saw on her cheek under the corner of her left eye and the gap between her two, porcelain front teeth. There was something very innocent and angelic looking about this woman, but there was also so much more. Her eyes were as blue as the deepest ocean and her skin was porcelain and flawless. The only thing off about the woman was the short, bob-style, mousy brown hair that crowned her magnificent face. Nikolai found himself wondering what the rest of her looked like and what her voice sounded like.

Artem chuckled lightly at Nikolai's reaction to the picture. He could empathize with his friend because he had felt the same way. "Extraordinary, right?"

"Da," Nikolai said, trying to find his voice. Shaking himself mentally, he closed the file and put it down. *Damn, it was just a picture!* Nikolai had been with many beautiful women, so what was so special about this one? Looking at Artem, he asked, "So what do we know? What type of relationship does she have with Paul?"

"Well, she's twenty-three and Paul's half-sister. They share the same mother, who was brutally murdered by Piper's stepfather when she was seven. Paul is about fifteen years older, so as far as we know, they never had a relationship. We've been told by informants that she has no idea who Paul is or that he's related to her. Piper also has no idea who her mother was."

"And who was that?"

"Lynn was the daughter of Texas oil tycoon, James Kaiser. The man was worth a little over two billion dollars and died of cancer a couple of weeks before Lynn was murdered. Piper's mother was Kaiser's only child and was disowned by him when she got into drugs and prostitution at the age of sixteen. Reports suggest that Lynn was clean off and on during her daughter's life, but that Kaiser only reached out to her when he knew he was dying. He apparently knew about Lynn's children and left his fortune to them. The money can only be accessed if the two of them sign for it together or Piper signs for it alone. I kind of feel bad for her, Niki. The woman was physically abused as a child, bounced around between foster homes, and raised in poverty with no idea about this money. Yet, despite her adversity, she graduated high school at the top of her class and summa cum laude from UNLV in pre-med. Looks and brains can be a deadly combination."

Nikolai sat and listened to Artem's words and felt an odd ache form in his chest. Now he understood why the mistrust was so prominent in her eyes. She was born to a drug addicted mother, raised in abuse and squalor, and had lost her entire family. Although he had lost his parents too, Nikolai had his brother Aleksandr and others who loved him dearly. He couldn't imagine what it would be like to grow up with only himself to depend upon. Piper's strong character and inner strength were evident by the fact that she was able to graduate and attend medical school. Knowing all of this, made Nikolai want the American even more. He loved a woman who was intelligent and could speak her mind.

"So, we know this young woman is in med school currently, and I imagine that takes up most of her time?" Nikolai asked, feeling his cock stir slightly in his pants. She was already making his body respond and he had not even met her. Typically, women didn't affect him like this, but something deep in Nikolai's core told him that this woman was different.

"One would think so, but to support herself, she works at a gentlemen's BDSM club called Sinner's Delight."

"Sinner's Delight?" Nikolai chuckled. "What the hell kind of name is that? What does she do there, exactly?"

"She's an exotic dancer. Rumor has it that she strips from time to time if the price is right. Celebrities and athletes alike frequent the club. Apparently, she is a big draw. Not sure if she works as a submissive or not, but we will find out."

"Interesting," Nikolai said, deep in thought, rubbing his clean-shaven jaw. This little bit of information further explained the hard glint of emotion he saw in her blue eyes. He knew the type of men who frequented clubs like that and how they treated the women inside. The women he had met in the BDSM clubs who came from those same environments, were typically hardened and very cynical. There was little soft-ness, and they rarely demonstrated their true emotions. The younger Volkov was not attracted to women like that, so the chances of a sexual relationship with Piper was out of the question, especially if she was similar in character. Maybe this young woman was different somehow. She clearly was using the club as a sort of steppingstone for a brighter future. If she stripped for these wealthy men, did she sleep with them as well? Nikolai hated to admit it, but the thought of this beau-tiful woman being with another man, made his blood boil. "Do we know for sure she engages in this type of activity?"

"Nyet, but we will once Peter calls us back," Artem said, referring to one of their top informants.

Hearing his phone ring, Nikolai picked it up immediately. After a moment of listening, he hung up and said to his friend. "Oleg Chechen just approached Zan in a crowded restaurant. He's taking the bastard downtown to the warehouse as we speak. I'm sorry, friend, but I have to go. Zan wants me to head to the club and babysit his new attorney." Nikolai then stood up as his personal guard Mikhas appeared out of nowhere. Nodding to the giant, the bratva guard knew exactly what his leader wanted. Looking at Artem once more, he said, "I want every piece of information you have on Piper sent to me immediately. I'll call Peter and speak with him personally."

"You got it, Niki. Say hello to Sophia for me."

Nikolai chuckled lightly before he turned and headed out of Artem's office. Before leaving, he turned to smile. "The meal was delicious, friend. Oh, and just so you know, if Piper does come back to Russia, she belongs to me." He then exited the room.

Chapter 3

Nikolai lay back on the mound of pillows as he sat on the bed in his private jet. Finishing a business report, he closed the laptop and put it to the side. He rubbed his flat, muscular stomach before he placed his hands behind his dark head and stretched out his tired frame. It was about two am Moscow time and his plane had been in the air for about an hour. Nikolai was flying to Las Vegas to meet Piper Williamson and hopefully help her acquire the money before killing Paul Morrison and Grecoff Chechen. Mikhas and a handful of elite guards sat in a separate living space on the plane, discussing their plan once they landed. Nikolai, on the other hand, had been unable to sleep since his brother Aleksandr was arrested for Viktor's death. Although his brother was safe back home and the truth was exposed, Nikolai still worried about his sibling. Truth be told, there would be no Nikolai without Aleksandr.

A smile spread across his face as he thought about Zan. Even though he was several years younger than his brother, the two had always been extremely close. He loved Aleksandr more than words could express and was glad that his brother was finally involving him in bratva business. For so long, the older Volkov had attempted to protect him from anything associated with the mafia, but Aleksandr had realized just how difficult that was. He had ensured that Nikolai graduated high school, gone to college, and lived a semi-normal life. The older Volkov had trained him at an early age how to fight and handle weapons. Now Nikolai was going to lead Viktor's bratva, and there was no way in hell he would let his brother down. Aleksandr had his hands full with his own business, bratva, and now a woman he knew would become his sister-in-law. He had never seen his brother as the type to settle down, but Aleksandr clearly felt something for Sophia. Aleksandr had yet to verbally profess his love for the redhead, but Nikolai saw it in his eyes.

Closing his own a moment, Nikolai groaned as Piper's image appeared in his mind. Since seeing the woman's photo, he had not been able to get her out of his head. After spending time talking to Sophia last night at Club Carnage, Nikolai had sexually dominated two blonde submissives who were similar in build to the woman he was going to help. He had always been partial to blondes, but there was something about Piper that was exciting and different. The one thing that irritated him about the whole situation was the way his body was responding to a woman he had never met. It was not like he lacked for female companionship, quite the opposite. Women flocked to him and he had several female friends. Quite frankly, Nikolai simply loved women and women loved him. He never led them on, and all were clear on where they stood with him emotionally. Unlike Aleksandr, Nikolai saw himself settling down one day and having children, however, he had no plans to do so anytime soon.

Picking up the file on Piper that lay beside his laptop,

Nikolai pulled out her picture again. The woman really was impressive to look at. He had talked to Peter via the phone about an hour ago, and the informant had confirmed the information Artem had shared with him, except for the young woman being a stripper. Nikolai also learned that Paul and Grecoff had visited her at the club a couple weeks ago but had flown to Texas immediately after. He had no doubts that they would be back to see Piper, but it would be extremely difficult for them since she was now being guarded 24/7 by his men. No one knew for sure what Paul and Grecoff had said to Piper, but his men reported that she now had a small cut on her cheek. If there was one thing the Volkov boys absolutely despised, it was violence toward women and these men would pay dearly for that crime.

Picking up his phone from the bedside table, Nikolai scrolled through additional files that Peter had sent him. Pulling up one simply marked "damn", Nikolai opened it. It was a video of Piper dressed provocatively in a slinky dress, dancing on stage for a handful of men. The gorgeous brunette was dressed in a red latex dress that zipped up the front and pushed up her large breasts. She also wore spiky, black heels and a red mask across her eyes. Her body was shapely, defined, and mirrored an hourglass. He zoomed in on the picture and allowed his eyes to travel her plump, perfect breasts, narrow waist, and wide, apple-shaped bottom. He felt his soft cock immediately begin to stir as he moaned internally. Piper's body was deliciously tantalizing, and the woman was a goddess he couldn't wait to see up close and personal.

Feeling his massive cock begin to throb, Nikolai fought the urge to stroke himself. What the hell was wrong with him? He prided himself on control as a dominant and frequently denied his own pleasure to please his submissives. The younger Volkov had not masturbated to a woman since he was a lad, so why was the urge so strong now? The more he looked at her pictures, the harder his erection became. Nikolai hated that he could not see her eyes through the mask, but he could imagine them watching him intently as he ate her pussy. Clenching his jaw together tightly, he shifted uncomfortably at the thought of Piper spread out before him like a sacrificial offering. As the need to find a release grew more and more intense, he clicked off the phone and stared at the ceiling as he tried to even his breathing.

Grabbing a t-shirt, Nikolai threw it on and cursed softly as he jumped out of the bed. He was so irritated with himself right now for his behavior. He was thirty years old, not twelve, seeing his first naked woman. Letting out a low, agitated growl, Nikolai headed toward the liquor cabinet. Vodka would help him get this stunning creature off his mind and so would a game of cards with the boys. Grabbing the bottle of clear liquid, he left the bedroom and found his men sitting around the table talking. Taking a seat at the head of it, he motioned for a glass and was slid one. He then poured himself a drink and quickly downed its contents.

"That's better," Nikolai said out loud, rolling his neck. *There is no way in hell a woman will ever control a Volkov. Now get your shit together, man.*

"Everything all right, Pakhan?" Mikhas asked, watching his bratva leader curiously. "You look a little on edge. Did something happen?"

"Nothing for you to worry about." He half-smiled, taking another drink. "Have you and our men figured out the plan for when we touch down in Las Vegas?"

"Da, we've already contacted the guards on the ground. When we land, you and I will head straight to Ms. Williamson's house. There might be one little snag, though."

"And that would be?"

"She has a roommate," the Russian guard responded as he

began dealing out cards to initiate a game. Looking at Nikolai, he asked, "Want in?"

Nodding his head yes, his thoughts drifted to Piper. Did she have a boyfriend? God, he hoped not. "Do we know if this roommate is male or female?"

"Not sure. The roommate's name is Andy Brennan. I would assume it's a man, but I guess it could be a woman. I can ask the men on the ground if it's important."

"It's not. We'll cross that bridge when we come to it," Nikolai replied offhandedly, inwardly stewing with irritation. As he picked up his cards, he told himself that he was glad she potentially had a boyfriend. That cooled his desire for the woman but did the opposite for his anger. *This is business, Nik,* he told himself. *You will go and help this woman and then kill your enemies. After that, you will head back home.* Needing to forget her momentarily, he motioned to the flight attendant for some drinks. It was going to be a long plane ride to America.

Five thousand miles away in Las Vegas, Piper was folding towels and putting them back into the laundry basket. She sat in the floor Indian style and was dressed comfortably in a black pair of yoga leggings, fuzzy socks, and a pink UNLV sweatshirt. Her curly blonde hair was pulled back in a ponytail and a box of half-eaten pizza sat beside her on the coffee table. She hummed along to the song on the radio before she picked up her Coke and took a drink. She was so engrossed in the music and her chore that she didn't hear Andy entering their apartment with the groceries.

"Piper, I'm home!" Andy yelled as she dropped her car keys on the small table by the door and walked into the kitchen.

The blonde hopped up off the floor to find her stepsister.

She immediately walked up to the grocery bag sitting on the table and peeked inside. "Did you get my Double Stuff Oreos?"

"You know I did, heifer. I don't understand how the hell you stay so fit with as many cookies as you eat. Makes me jealous." Andy smiled as she watched Piper grab the cookies out of the bag and prop herself up on the kitchen counter. "Did Jonathan call? He said something about us going out tonight, but I haven't heard from him."

"Sorry, babe. Been home all day and nothing," Piper replied, pulling off one side of the cookie. As she began licking the sweet, white filling, she asked, "Why are you still dating that loser? He is so inconsiderate to you, D."

"I'll admit he can be a jerk sometimes, but I like him. If you would take the time to get to know him instead of judging him, you would see that. Plus, you can't deny how hot he is! You know I like my men big, tall, and tattooed."

"Yeah, yeah, I know." Piper smiled, rolling her eyes as she watched Andy put away the groceries. The woman before her was not only her stepsister but a mother of sorts. She also thought the tall, plus-sized woman was the most beautiful woman on the planet. Andy had black hair, cut in a short, bob style that framed her face, and eyes the color of warm honey. She also was assertive, loud, and not afraid to speak her mind. She was very smart and had just finished veterinarian school. Piper thanked God every day that Andy had come into her life when she was eighteen, because things would have been much harder without her help.

"So how did your exam go yesterday? I know we live together, but I feel like I haven't really talked to you in weeks."

"I aced the written exam, however, the clinical part didn't go well," The blonde said with a huff as she pulled out another Oreo cookie to eat. "Remember me telling you about the Dr. Shaw situation?"

"That's the doctor who flunked you during a clinical, right? He recognized you as a dancer at the club?"

"One and the same. Well, the asshole flunked me during another procedure yesterday, that, might I add, I had already passed with flying colors. The whole time I was doing it, he was trying to look down my blouse. He even tried to brush up against my chest a couple of time. The worst part was that he made a point to do it in front of my peers."

Knowing her sister's temper and wicked, verbal comebacks, Andy asked, "And what was your response?"

"I told him I was surprised he could see the mistakes I was making since his eyes and hands were focused on my breasts." Piper smiled sweetly, reenacting her demeanor during the encounter. "Shaw turned ten shades of red and began yelling at me in front of everyone. I was pulled aside and verbally reprimanded by Dr. Stevens, who assured me that something like that would never happen again and that Shaw would be dealt with."

"Well, at least the lead clinical director is on your side."

"Yeah, well, we'll see for how long. I don't trust him, either. I heard from a couple of third year residents that he's a chauvinist, too, who likes to prey on young med students. Hopefully, he does what he says and I won't have to deal with Shaw again. Anyway, enough about me. How are things going at work?"

Piper ate her cookies as she listened to her stepsister talk about work. So much had changed in her life since she had encountered Paul and Grecoff two weeks ago. She hated to admit it, but she was terrified. Her fingers unconsciously stroked the small cut that was healing on her face where the foreign man had slapped her. Grecoff had been wearing a large stone, ruby ring that had made the small mark, but it was now scabbed over and no longer hurt. When the men let her leave, she had run back to the dressing room and hid in the bathroom. Once there, she had slid down against the wall and cried her eyes out. After breaking down, Piper had immediately gone to Al and told him what happened. To his credit, Al tried to locate the two men and had even called the police, but neither man could be found. When she had told Andy the story, her stepsister had totally freaked out and bought a gun. She had even signed them up for a firearm course. Piper insisted that they find a new apartment asap because the last thing she wanted was Paul and Grecoff showing up at her home.

"Earth to Piper. Are you listening to me?" Andy asked, hating the look she saw on the younger woman's face. She knew her thoughts had drifted to the attack at the club and although she had tried to cheer the blonde up, she just hadn't been the same. When Piper finally looked at her, there was a great sadness in her eyes. Walking up to the younger woman, she tucked a strand of platinum blonde hair behind her ear and stroked her cheek. "I knew the moment you drifted off, babe. I wish you would stop worrying about those two guys. There is no way in hell that I am going to let them hurt you."

"I'm sorry, D," she sighed, putting her half-eaten cookie back in the bag. Meeting Andy's eyes, she asked, "Did you get a chance to look at that apartment today?"

"I did. It's really nice. I'm just worried that it might be a little too expensive, especially since you are quitting the club."

"I can always take extra shifts at the hospital if I need to or maybe I can just do private dances at the club—"

"You are done with the club, Piper," Andy said sternly, putting her hand over the blonde's mouth. "You didn't let me finish what I was going to say. We are moving soon. I really liked the apartment; I just want to double check the figures and make sure we can afford it and still have plenty of money for other things. I don't want you working full time plus, while being a resident in med school. You are going to need down time at some point."

"I didn't mean to cut you off. I'm just so scared that those men are going to come back and finish what they started," Piper replied sadly, feeling the unshed tears filling her eyes.

"Just let those bastards try. I'll shoot them dead before they even get in the door," Andy barked, hugging her stepsister protectively. "Don't you worry, babe. I got you. I promise I won't let anyone hurt you."

"I just can't shake the feeling that I am going to see them again. For the life of me, I just don't understand what in the hell they wanted. I have gone over the questions they asked me a thousand times and can't figure out why they wanted to know about my family. Maybe Mom was in some sort of trouble when she died? I mean, I know she had issues with drugs and relapsed heavily before Maury killed her, but maybe there was something else."

"If that's true, then why wait sixteen years? Guys like that don't wait that long to collect a debt. Maybe they realized you were not who they thought you were."

"But Grecoff said he would be back!" Piper exclaimed, grabbing Andy's hand. "I pissed this guy off, although I didn't mean to. He wants to hurt me, D. I saw it deep in his eyes."

"Like I told you earlier, babe, there is no way in hell I am going to let this guy near you. I wish I could have been there to help you when this happened. I'm sorry I let you down, but that won't happen again."

"You have no reason to be sorry. I don't blame you for anything. These guys would not only hurt me, but they would hurt you, and I can't let that happen. I just don't know how to deal with this. Hopefully, I'm not the person they were looking for."

"You can't be! I mean, you're a poor college student who came from one of the most dysfunctional families on the planet. Your mom was a junkie who didn't have two pennies to rub together, for crying out loud. Hell, you don't even know who your father was. Maybe one of the VIPs is in trouble. I mean, you've told me that they tell you intimate secrets sometimes."

Piper said nothing in response as she pulled another cookie out of the package and began to nibble on it. Innately, she knew those men had nothing to do with her clients and that it had all been about her. Like she told Andy, Piper had gone through the questions in her mind multiple times. Why had they centered on her mother? There had to be something about her past, but what in the hell could men from another country want with that information? Her mother had no money and they had lived off assistance from the state. Due to her mother's drug habit, they had bounced between shelters until Maury had come into the picture. Although he was severely abusive to them, he had at least provided them with steady housing. Maybe something had happened with her mother before she had been born. She vaguely remembered Lynn talking about wealthy men when she was high, but Piper had no idea what that was about. She had been so young at the time and had not focused on her mother's rantings. Oh, how Piper wished she knew that information now.

"Listen, I think it's extremely weird that they were asking about your family, but they saw how little you know. Maybe that was enough for these men. I wish I could ease your mind, but just know if these jackasses come back, they won't walk out alive. If that means going to jail, then just call me Big Bertha and put me in stripes."

"Well, Bertha, at least you look good in stripes," Piper replied, cracking a smile, attempting to lighten the mood a little. "However, remember orange is the new black. That's not really your color."

"You see this?" Andy scoffed, giving Piper the middle

finger. When the blonde chuckled, Andy put her arm around Piper's neck and pressed their foreheads together. "I love you, sis. I know you're scared, but we'll fight this together. They took you away from me when Lynn died. They won't do it again."

"No, they won't, and don't worry, I love you too." Piper smiled as the two hugged each other. Playfully pushing the taller woman away, she said, "Now enough of this mushy crap. What are you cooking us for dinner tonight?"

"Nothing, because we are going out."

"Out? No way. I have a clinical in the morning. I can't get drunk, D."

"I'm not saying get drunk. I say we grab a burger at Mama's, gamble a little bit on the strip, and then head over to Pulse and dance the rest of the night away. We haven't gone out like that in a long time. Come on, we'll have fun. It will take your mind off everything."

"How dare you hit me with my favorite things!" Piper smiled, with mock upset. "Look, while an evening out sounds amazing, I don't want to have to deal with a bunch of dudes coming on to me."

"You won't have to worry about that. We'll be on our honeymoon tonight," Andy replied as she held Piper's hand and got down on one knee.

"Get up!" The blonde laughed loudly as Andy joined in and got to her feet.

"So, what's it going to be?"

"Fine!" Piper chuckled, rolling her eyes playfully as she jumped off the counter. "But we honeymoon in the Maldives. Got it?"

"You got it, bitch!" Andy laughed, slapping Piper on the butt playfully. "Now go finish the laundry and take a shower. I got some budgeting to do before we go out tonight."

The blue-eyed goddess quickly headed back to the living

room to finish the laundry. She really didn't want to go out tonight, but she did want to get her mind off her troubles. Plus, Club Pulse had ridiculous security and most of the men there were her friends. Piper could ask any of them for help and would if she needed to. Letting out a sigh, she sat back in the floor. She was going to make herself enjoy tonight, even if it meant pretending for Andy's sake.

Chapter 4

Nikolai approached the small, Vegas apartment with Mikhas at his side. It was early morning in Nevada and their plane had just touched down. As the two men walked up to the door, they were met by another bratva guard who let them into the condo. When Nikolai entered the tiny space, he scanned his surroundings. He couldn't believe that two people lived here. The entire apartment was half the size of his master bedroom but had a very modern, feminine feel. Piper and her roommate clearly liked cleanliness and he could smell a light, flowery scent in the air that Nikolai hoped belonged to the woman he was coming to help. As he walked from room to room, he took in the multitude of pictures on the wall and shelves and was mesmerized by how attractive Piper was. The young woman clearly was close to her roommate Andy, whom he had learned was a woman, because the two appeared close and happy in photos. They also were not a stranger to hard work and determination and Nikolai admired that greatly. Both women had accolades of their accomplishments around the apartment proudly on display. Piper was not only physically beautiful, but he could tell she was both intelligent and emotionally strong.

Walking back into the living room, Mikhas met Nikolai just as he hung up his cell phone. "The ladies are getting ready to leave a club called Pulse. However, they are not coming home together. Andy is leaving with a man who is presumed to be her boyfriend and Piper is heading home."

Nikolai nodded before he sat down on the brown, leather sofa and casually crossed his legs. He was dressed for business in a black, Brioni suit with a white linen shirt underneath and no tie. He had one goal and that was to talk to Piper and keep her safe. Nikolai had no doubts that Piper wouldn't believe his claims, so he brought a briefcase full of files to convince her. Although he was physically attracted to her, Nikolai had no intentions of sleeping with her. He wanted to keep their relationship strictly business, at least at first. Maybe once he killed Grecoff and Paul, Nikolai would attempt to woo her.

Feeling Mikhas sit down beside him on the couch, Nikolai asked, "So, what do you think of Las Vegas, friend? I know you have not had an opportunity to explore the city or its women yet but hopefully you will have some free time."

"Meh." Mikhas shrugged, kicking back to rest his tired, large frame. "I would rather be back in my homeland, honestly, but duty calls. America can keep its women as well. They all seem so complicated with their problems, not simple like Russian women."

"Russian women are far from simple, Mik, and you know it." Nikolai chuckled in response. "You can't deny that the women over here are just as beautiful as ours."

"They are beautiful but... fake," Mikhas replied with a distorted face, making the shape of a woman with his hands. "I mean, it's hard to tell if their parts are real or not. Russian women, like Katja, are all-woman and soft."

"That's just because you like Katja," Nikolai responded,

the smile not fading from his full, pink lips. Mikhas was second in command when it came to the guards but also one of his best friends. The man was in love with Nikolai's submissive, Katja, but wouldn't verbally admit it. The two had slept together a few times and Nikolai had offered his mistress to Mikhas full time but the guard always refused. "Are you ever going to tell her just how much you like her?"

"Nyet," Mikhas said, shaking his head. "No woman will ever come between our friendship or my loyalty to you, Nik. Besides, Katja is in love with you. She is also one of your favorite submissives."

"Katja is one of my favorites, Mikhas, but I don't love her. I care for her as a person, but it goes no further than that. She also isn't in love with me. Katja is a hopeless romantic, my friend, you know that. I've told you countless times, she's yours if you want. I don't think she would object. She frequently mentions you as someone she could see herself settling down with."

"Really?" Mikhas asked in surprise as he thought about the lovely Katja. "She has never mentioned that to me."

"She wouldn't because she fears rejection, the same as you. Look, your birthday is coming up in a few weeks. If Katja is okay with it, she will now belong to you."

"Nik I can't do that. I—

"You can, and you will. That's an order, not a request," Nikolai replied sternly, waving his finger at Mikhas. He could tell his friend was more than pleased by the wide grin on his face.

"Thank you, Nik. I can never repay you for your kindness," Mikhas said softly. He loved Nikolai like a brother and respected the man greatly. Mikhas was a couple of years older than Nikolai and had worked for the Volkovs for the last fifteen years. In that time, he had grown close to not only Nikolai, but Aleksandr as well.

"You repay me daily, Mik." Nikolai grinned. "Just remember to name one of your children after me, okay?"

Mikhas chuckled loudly just as one of the guards approached him and whispered in his ear. When the man walked away, he looked at Nikolai and said, "The woman is two minutes away. Excuse me. I need to make sure everyone is in place."

"Are there any weapons we should be aware of?"

"There was a gun in the drawer beside you, but that has already been taken. It appears that Piper was affected greatly by Paul and Grecoff's visit because the weapons were acquired after that."

Nikolai nodded and closed his eyes a minute as he silently seethed with rage. He knew Piper had been afraid, but if she was buying weapons, the woman had been terrified. He had several reasons to kill Paul and Grecoff and those began with his brother but now Piper added another dimension to his hate for them. He uncrossed his legs and sat forward on the couch. Although he didn't understand why, Nikolai found himself getting nervous waiting for Piper's arrival. The woman appeared one way in pictures, but they only captured moments in one's life. Everything in her file suggested that she was innocent and needed help, but he didn't know her. Seeing the motion sensor light kicking on outside, he was about to find out.

Walking up the sidewalk to her apartment, Piper stifled a yawn. Glancing at her watch, she could not believe it was almost three in the morning. She was tired but she'd had a good time out with Andy. After eating her favorite food, the two gambled a little and then ended up in the nightclub. They had danced and flirted with a group of bankers, until Andy's boyfriend Jonathan had showed up and taken away her step-sister's attention. She was not only tired but feeling a little warm as well. She had initially decided not to drink but had quickly gotten caught up in the shots that began flowing like water. Piper knew deep down it wasn't safe to drink with Paul and Grecoff out there, but she had wanted to forget her troubles at least for a minute. It had helped to know that she was surrounded by large, body-building men who were her friends and would hopefully protect her. Now, the only thing she wanted to do was get on some comfy pajamas and crawl into bed. After all, she had clinicals in just a few hours and needed to at least rest her eyes a little.

Once Piper reached the door, she fumbled in her purse for her keys. After unlocking the door and walking inside, she dropped her purse on the table and closed it. When she turned around, her ocean blue eyes widened in fear half a second before she grabbed the bat out of the hallway closet and charged at him. As she swung the wood at him, Nikolai stood up and stopped the bat from hitting him with his hand. He then jerked it out of her hand and tossed it to the side. Piper then threw herself at him to viciously assault him, but before she could begin, he had her turned around in his arms and placed in a bear hug. She struggled against him and tried to stomp on his feet and head butt him, but the man moved with the swiftness and agility of a cheetah and she was defenseless against his size and strength.

"Calm down, Piper," Nikolai urged, attempting to comfort the gorgeous blonde. He could feel her heart beating wildly and knew she was terrified although she chose to fight him. "I don't want to hurt you."

"Let go of me, you son of a bitch!" she screamed, trying everything in her power to get out of his vise-like hold. Her nails scratched at his muscular forearms as she jerked her body, trying to break free from his hold, but nothing she did seemed to be working.

"Stop fighting me, dammit," Nikolai growled between clenched teeth as he held her tightly. The woman was stronger than he had suspected she would be. He could feel a small trail of blood running down one arm. "I have no intention of hurting you. I just want to talk."

"Go to hell!" Piper yelled fearfully, but she was oddly calmed by the deep, rich, masculine sound coming from his chest. She also was enveloped by the heavenly, light earthy scent of damp wood and spices. However, as good as the stranger smelled, he had the same accent as the man called Grecoff and she assumed that this guy worked for him. "Let me go please!"

"I'll let you go as soon as you calm down. Now stop struggling," the bratva leader commanded, his voice strong and even-tempered. He knew the woman was afraid of him and wanted to reassure her that he wouldn't hurt her. When her struggling began to decrease, he said in her ear, "I know you were hurt by two men recently, Piper, one of whom sounded like me. I promise you that I am not associated with Grecoff. As I said initially, I only want to help you."

"You don't even know me," Piper popped back, trying to fight the tears that threatened to fall down her face. Then as his words began to soak in, she asked, "How the hell do you know about the men who attacked me if you're not associated with them?"

"I plan on explaining everything to you, but I want to know that we can talk rationally," he stated calmly, closing his eyes a moment as he tried not to focus on her plump, apple-shaped bottom rubbing against his groin. He inhaled her sweet, soft, feminine scent and was immediately transported to a field of pink and white peonies that he used to run in as a child. When he felt her body relax against him further, he asked. "If I let you go, can we talk quietly and calmly?"

Trying to level her own emotions, the American woman took several deep breaths. Maybe the man holding her really did want to talk. Even though he was holding her tightly, she had felt him shift his body intentionally so he wouldn't crush her. Plus, there was something in his voice that instinctually told her that this man was telling her the truth about talking. His demeanor was different than Paul and Grecoff's had been at the club. At least if she calmed herself down and he let her go, she might have a chance to escape. Just at that moment, Piper saw another giant of a man move to stand in front of the door and knew that thought was over before it even began. Letting out a loud sigh, Piper nodded her head and felt the hold he had on her ease.

Nikolai nodded to Mikhas to be on alert as he released Piper and she jumped from his grip to look between him and his second in command. As she looked back and forth, his body was unprepared for a full view of Piper. He stifled a groan as his grey eyes traveled over her supple, delicious body that was covered in a navy blue, backless, spaghetti-strapped dress. The silky material hugged her narrow waist and wide hips and displayed toned, bronzed legs that disappeared into delicate, cream-colored, six-inch heels. Curly hair that was almost platinum in color and as soft as rose petals hung midway down her back and kept her long, slender neck and shoulders concealed from him. He liked the blonde hair much better than that brown haircut in the pictures. Damn, her body was pure perfection! The pictures and video he had seen of her had been extraordinary but nothing had prepared Nikolai for the real thing.

Realizing the man at the door was clearly taking orders from the one who was holding her just a moment ago, she turned around to face Nikolai. She found herself unable to breath when her eyes touched the massive, gorgeous specimen before her. Everything about this man screamed of wealth, power, and danger, but oh, how Piper longed for just a small taste of what he could offer. The man was much taller than she was and as wide and solid as a brick wall. His face was deeply tanned and clean-shaven, but the most haunting thing about him was his steel grey eyes. Her body flushed hotly, and her clit began to pulse wildly as his eyes roamed over her before lifting to her face. Shaking herself mentally as she let out an exasperated sigh, Piper pulled her attention away from him and looked toward the drawer of the end table where they kept their gun. If she could get to it, Piper could possibly turn the tables.

"The gun is no longer there, Piper," Nikolai said, reading her thoughts. When her eyes met his, he said, "We've already secured it, so no need to try anything stupid. Also, my men are surrounding the apartment so I wouldn't suggest trying to run, either."

"Who are you, and what the hell do you want from me?" Piper yelled, wrapping her arms around herself as she broke eye contact.

"My name is Nikolai Volkov, and the man behind you is Mikhas Verenich. I am not only a businessman, but I am the leader of a bratva in Russia. The two men who came to see you are not only my enemies, but yours. They are coming back to either kidnap you or kill you, and I want to assure you that I will keep you safe and protected," Nikolai replied, watching her intensely. He could see unfallen tears in her deep blue eyes, but there was no way she was going to shed them. "I know you're confused and have a thousand questions, and I plan on answering them all. Come have a seat. There is a lot we need to discuss."

"Can I have a moment to myself?" Piper asked, rubbing her bare arm as a chill shot up her back. She didn't know what it was, but she loved the way her name fell from his lips. She must be drunker than she thought because his words and demeanor were comforting to her somehow. She had even thought she had seen a brief flash of empathy in his grey eyes as he spoke to her. Piper had feared Paul and Grecoff, but she didn't get the same sensation from Nikolai.

"You've got five minutes."

Piper nodded before she headed into the kitchen. When she walked over to the phone to pick it up and make a call, she saw Mikhas immediately appear and block her ability to do so. She stepped back and crossed her arms over her chest before she leaned over the sink to give herself time to think. Nikolai claimed he was there to protect her from Paul and Grecoff, but she knew instinctually that the information they had involved her family's past somehow. Piper had wanted to know the truth about who she was for so long, and now that she stood on the precipice of that knowledge, she was terrified of what she might find. Looking out into the living room, she was not surprised to see Nikolai watching her intently. The way his eyes traveled slowly over her body, had a hot, electrical current racing up her spine. Nikolai had a face that was heaven personified and a body that was so big and strong. Could this man really know who she was and where her family was from? Could he protect her from those dangerous men? *The only way to find out is to sit and talk to him,* Piper thought to herself. *You have an internal truth detector and will know if he's lying. If he is, then you can try to run.*

Making her way back into the living room, she straightened her back regally and threw back her head. "Okay, we can talk, but we do so at the dining room table. Understand?"

Nikolai cocked a dark brow at her as a slow smile spread across his lips. The afraid, little kitten was now attempting to show him her claws, and he liked it. Without a word, he stood up and walked toward the table with her. After she took a seat, he then unbuttoned his suit jacket and sat down beside the blonde. In Russian, he said over his shoulder, "Call and book the Sky Villa at the Palms. I want the entire floor and as many suites as we need on the floor directly below us. Also, have a car waiting outside for us. I'm not sure how long this will take, but I do know that she will be coming with us."

Piper watched Mikhas quickly disappear out of the room. Looking directly at Nikolai, she asked, "What did you just say to him? Where is he going?"

"He'll be back in just a few minutes. I told him to get us a room here in Vegas tonight. We just landed about an hour ago and I have not had an opportunity to locate a hotel."

Piper didn't know whether or not to believe what he was saying so she barked, "Well, from now on, you speak English. I want to know every word that is being said from this point forward."

"Let me make one thing abundantly clear," Nikolai said in a calm, firm voice, although internally, he was seething. He had never had anyone, let alone a woman, yell orders at him the way she was. There was no way in hell he was going to allow the disrespect to continue. "I dictate what happens here tonight, not you. If there is something that you would like to say to me, you will do so using a respectful, calm tone. You are in no position to make any type of demands and I sincerely doubt that you want to see me upset. Do you understand?"

She couldn't hold his intense, heated gaze as she nodded her head in agreement and looked away. What the hell was she doing upsetting a man who was double her size and extremely dangerous? Why was her clitoris twitching in her panties painfully at the way he took command? Piper was so confused at the opposing feelings between her head and the rest of her body. However, she didn't want to make him angry, and deep down something told her that this man would do exactly what he said he would.

"Good. Now let's proceed," the Russian replied, hiding his smile at her submissiveness. Pulling a file out of his briefcase, he began, "As I told you initially, my name is Nikolai, and I am the leader of a bratva."

"What is a bratva?" Piper interjected, cutting him off.

"A bratva is a family run organization that controls a large part of the underbelly of Russia. However, several of us also have our hands in legitimate business ventures."

"So, you're like the mafia? You're a criminal?"

"If that's how you can relate to what a bratva is, then, yes, we are like that. However, I can assure you that my brother and I are far from criminal. You make assumptions about me based on what little knowledge you have. We don't deal in drugs or prostitution and we don't kill people just for the hell of it. We do, however, demand loyalty and honesty from every member. Again, not all bratvas are like ours and this leads to men like Paul and Grecoff."

"The two men who came here, right?"

"Da." Nikolai nodded. "Grecoff is the head of a bratva, but Paul is not. He married into one, though, but killed his father-in-law, who was the head of that family. Paul is working with Grecoff to gain power and influence in the underworld. The reason they came to see you is because you have access to a large sum of money that Paul needs."

"Money?" she scoffed harshly. "I don't have any money, and I sure as hell have no idea why this dude would be visiting me. He must have me confused with someone else."

"Paul came to you because he is your half-brother," Nikolai said softly while he watched a range of emotions cross her angelic face as he passed her the file folder. "You have access to a large fortune, Piper; you just don't know about it. He needs you to get that fortune."

Without opening the file, she looked at him and said, "I don't understand. The only money I have is what I've worked for. My family was poor, and my mom passed away when I was seven. I—"

"Your mother wasn't honest with you about your family, sweetheart," Nikolai interjected. He hated the overwhelming emotion he saw in her transparent blue eyes. Although Nikolai knew the information he possessed would be hard to hear, he wanted to be upfront and honest with this woman. "Your mother, Lynn Williamson, was an only child. Her father, James Kaiser, was a Texas oil tycoon. Your mother developed a bad drug addiction when she was about sixteen and began prostituting herself. Once your grandfather found out what she was doing, he disowned her. Paul was the result of a brief marriage she had with a young senator. When this man divorced your mother, her drug addiction worsened, and she was put in jail for a few years on theft and prostitution charges. After being released, she stayed clean for a while then got pregnant with you. Paul, as far as we know, never saw your mother again after she divorced his father."

Piper sat there in stunned silence as Nikolai talked. She felt so many conflicting emotions as she thought about her mother. If what this man said was true, why in the hell didn't her mother tell her this? They had lived in squalor and filth and there had been many times when she had gone hungry because her mom had blown the money on drugs. If it had not been for Andy or neighbors, she probably would have starved to death. Also, Paul was her half-brother? She had not gotten brotherly vibes from the man, and it now made sense why. She wanted to cry from the overwhelming stress and anxiety she was feeling, but there was no way she was going to break down in front of a total stranger.

"I'm sorry that you have to learn about your family this way," he said softly. "I know this is a lot to take in, but I want to make one thing clear to you. Paul may be biologically related to you, but he doesn't want a relationship."

"Yeah, I figured that out already," the blonde replied sarcastically, only to see his dark brow arch. Lowering her eyes, she said in a softer tone, "I don't want a relationship with Paul, either, nor do I plan on dying because of a little money tucked away somewhere."

"Sweetheart, this is no small amount of money we're talking about. Try half a billion dollars."

"Half a billion dollars? Yeah, right." Piper laughed coldly. "And you flew all the way here to help me get it, free of charge?"

"Yes," he responded simply. He could tell she didn't believe a word he was saying. "I understand your hesitation and mistrust, but Paul is a despicable, low life who not only killed a man I considered a father, but he tried to destroy my brother. Paul and the Grecoffs have been a thorn in my family's side for a long time, and they deserve to pay for what they've done. I'm tired of watching innocent people die. He will kill you once he acquires the money."

"If I give Paul the money, why would he kill me? I'm not going to tell anyone about what happened. I mean, money like that would change my life, but why should I believe you? You've already told me that you're some sort of mafia guy. Men like that don't help women like me for free, and there is no way in hell that I am going to pay a debt on my back."

Nikolai cracked his thick neck in annoyance. Damn, this woman had a sharp tongue! He wanted to beat the woman's ass and was fighting for control of his emotions. Women didn't talk to him like this, and he would be damned if he allowed her to continue her uncooperative, obstinate attitude. Standing up, he calmly leaned over her. One of his large hands rested on the back of her chair and the other rested on the table in front of her. He found himself secretly enjoying the way her body trembled as she swallowed the lump in her throat and craned her neck to look at him. His eyes were darkened with anger and his voice was laced with stern, quiet dominance as he said, "If I want you on your back, sweetheart, then that is exactly where you'll be. I have already warned you about your tone and attitude. Consider this moment right here your last and final warning. Now, do you think we can finish this conversation in a respectful, adult manner?"

"Y-yes," Piper whispered breathlessly as his lips moved closer to hers. God, he smelled wonderful and the current of electricity passing between the two of them was strong and palpable. This man scared and sexually excited her all at the same time. Her clit throbbed in her underwear with anticipation and need. The breath caught in her throat as she leaned in closer and brought her lips centimeters from his. However, just as her mouth touched his, Nikolai pulled back abruptly and sat back down. She let out a shaky exhale as she watched him mentally shake himself, grab his laptop, and begin typing on it. Piper lowered her own head a moment and screamed at herself internally. She had just tried to kiss a total stranger! What the hell was wrong with her?

He tried to level his racing heart as he typed on his keyboard. He was stunned that Piper had attempted to kiss him. Nikolai had wanted to crush his body to hers intimately but wanted to keep things professional at the same time. It had taken every ounce of control within him to pull back. He had lost himself for a moment in Piper's eyes, and that never happened. He would just have to make sure it didn't happen again. Flipping the laptop around so she could see it, he said, "Here is the account that contains the money. All it needs is your electronic signature and it's yours."

"But I thought you said Paul needed me to access it?" she asked in disbelief as she quickly scanned the information on the screen.

"He needs you. You don't need him," Nikolai corrected as

Piper manipulated the keys and scrolled through the pages. He watched a huge range of emotions cross her lovely face again as she read through the contents of the documents. "When you sign this, you dictate where the money goes, and every single cent will belong to you. The bank has set up an account where you can immediately access the money." Nikolai then reached into his suit jacket and pulled out a bank book, check book, and two credit cards and placed them on the table. "Here are the things you need to access the account. As you can see, it's in your name only. It's yours to do with what you will."

She didn't know what to say or how to react. The documentation looked legitimate and deep down, she knew Nikolai was telling her the truth. According to what she was looking at, she now had a half a billion dollars. This money would forever change her life! Fighting back tears that suddenly sprang to her eyes, she looked at him and said, "If this money is really mine, I want Andy to have half of it."

"If that is what you want, then you will be able to do that in the morning. I have already arranged for you to meet with my own personal accountant, who will be able to help you figure out what to do with such a large sum of money. Right now, I need you to pack a few things because you're coming with me to the hotel."

"What?" Piper asked as panic began to set in as he packed his briefcase and stood up. "Why do I have to go with you? I thought you said you didn't want anything from me. I thought—"

He held up his hand to silence her. "I don't want anything from you, but Paul and the Grecoff are going to realize that the money is missing and come after you. Until we dispose of them, I need to keep you safe. The only way I can do that is if I have eyes on you 24/7. When all of this is over, you can return home."

"Why can't I stay here? You clearly have men who can watch me."

"Because I can't personally watch you," Nikolai said as his large hand cupped her cheek gently, trying to comfort her. He was not surprised to feel skin as soft as the finest silk. He loved the way she turned her cheek into his palm. "Like it or not, sweetheart, you're my responsibility now. As soon as the threat is removed, things will go back to normal for you. If you are worried about where you will sleep, it will be in my suite, but you will have your own room."

"What about Andy? If something happened to her, I would never forgive myself."

"Andy will be kept safe, the same as you. I will have a team guarding her every move. I understand that she means a great deal to you and you will be allowed to talk to her as often as you like. Now I need you to pack a bag quickly. Mikhas will help you should you need it." He then released her before abruptly turning to leave the room.

Chapter 5

Piper followed Mikhas into the lavish, Palms Sky Villa as she took in her decadent surroundings. She had never seen anything quite so opulent before and the décor of the room was exquisite to view. She knew Nikolai was wealthy, based on the cut of his clothes, but this took things to a whole other level. Unfortunately, she had not seen the man in question since leaving their apartment. She still had several questions for him, although her body screamed for sleep. Was he avoiding her on purpose? Had he lied to her and was now changing things on her? It would be her luck that a man as gorgeous as the Russian turned out to be a total, dishonest loser. Glancing at the clock on the wall, Piper gasped loudly. It was almost five-thirty, and she was supposed to have class at eight. She was not only physically but emotionally drained as well. Although she felt exhausted, she didn't think she was going to be able to sleep.

"This is your room for the duration of your stay," Mikhas said, cutting through her thoughts as he set her bags on the floor. "As you can see, there is a small sitting area connected to the bedroom. Bathroom is down the hall. Nikolai will have his own private area on the second floor of the villa. He will be joining you a little later. If you need anything, I'm right across the hall in my own suite." He then watched her nod before she looked around the room and her eyes settled on the door of the villa. "Look, there is no way you are getting out of this room so get the thought out of your head. No one is going to hurt you here. All you need to do is calm down and relax. Think of your stay here like a holiday."

"Holiday, huh? Yeah, that's a great idea," she replied sarcastically, looking out the wall made of glass that consisted of the best view of Las Vegas in the entire city. It was really ironic that she have such a beautiful cage keeping her from freedom. When her eyes found his again, she asked, "Do you think I can call Andy? I left her a note, but I want her to hear my voice too, so she doesn't get scared. I'd like to keep my cell phone too."

"Nikolai will decide if you can keep your phone. Right now, you may have it to call your roommate. When you are done, you will give it back to me."

When Mikhas passed her the cell phone and stood there waiting for her to make the call, she barked in an irritated voice, "Can I at least have some privacy?"

"Nyet. You make call in front of me or make no call at all."

Piper huffed and fumed angrily as she found her stepsister in her contacts. She knew Andy was probably asleep and still with Jonathan. After leaving a detailed message about where she was and that she would contact her in the morning, she handed the phone back to Mikhas before he smiled at her and walked out of the room. Suddenly feeling very alone and over-whelmed, she let out a loud sigh and fought the tears that again threatened to fall down her face. She tried focusing on her amazing surroundings, but she could not get out of her own head. Since her brief meeting with Nikolai, Piper found herself overanalyzing tonight's events. Not only had she learned a little more about her past, but she was now a quarter of a billion dollars richer. She was also now locked in a high-priced dungeon with a man she didn't know, who was supposed to be protecting her from ruthless killers. Exhaling loudly, she felt trapped, and those feelings took her back to her childhood.

Thinking of her childhood, made Piper specifically think of her mother. Anger nearly suffocated her as she thought about all the times she had gone to bed hungry while her mother blew grocery money on drugs. How many times had she taken care of her mother when she was too out of it to function? How many times had Lynn allowed Maury to beat her and Andy and leave them in a sobbing puddle on the floor? It infuriated her that all that time, she had a potential lifeline in the form of a grandparent. She couldn't understand cutting a child from your life because they made mistakes, but she *really* couldn't understand sitting back and watching your innocent grandchildren go through abuse and starvation. Piper had no idea if she would have children one day, but she knew there was no way in hell that she would ever allow her children to be abused, let alone go hungry. Lynn knew her father was a billionaire, so why didn't she ever reach out to him for help? She had so many questions and the people who could answer them were all dead. She did know, however, that it was going to take some time to process what she learned tonight as well as her feelings about it.

Shaking herself mentally, Piper grabbed her bags and carried them into the bedroom before tossing them on the large bed. Pulling out a pair of cozy long-sleeve pajamas, she walked into the bathroom. She threw her hair up in a loose ponytail and quickly scrubbed her face before slipping on the comfy night clothes. She smoothed the fallen strands of platinum hair away from her face as she stared at herself in the mirror. Piper was so damn tired, but she needed to try and contact the clinical director before attempting to sleep. She wished she could talk to Nikolai about going to class but had no idea when she would see him again. She was still trying to understand her feelings regarding the dark-haired man. The blonde had wanted to hate the bratva leader but instead she found herself extremely attracted to him. He had been so kind to her tonight and had not tried to hurt her once. Deep down, she didn't feel threatened by him and innately she knew he was telling her the truth. Piper had been unprepared for the sympathy she had seen in his lovely grey eyes throughout their conversation and could tell he felt bad for her. *Oh well you can think about all of this in the morning* she sighed loudly. *Looks like you are going to have plenty of free time.* With the last thought she turned and headed back toward the bedroom. She gasped loudly when she ran into a massive wall of muscle and strength. Before she stumbled back and fell, Piper was caught in a pair of strong arms.

"Whoa there." Nikolai said in a deep, masculine voice as he steadied her movements. Feeling as if he had been shocked, he quickly released her only to find his eyes roaming over her voluptuous body. He had intentionally distanced himself after their initial meeting in the apartment because he found being close to her disturbing to his senses. Even now, standing with no makeup and simple pajamas, Piper was remarkable to look at. Nikolai wanted nothing more than to strip her down and lay her on the bed. He could not even begin to understand the barrage of emotions that raced through his body when she had attempted to kiss him. He had intended on seeing her again after she had time to sleep but found himself seeking her out. Nikolai wanted to ensure that Piper was okay and that she was feeling more comfortable, or at least that is what he told himself.

"Sorry about that. I didn't see you." She replied breathlessly, casting her eyes down nervously. He stood before her in a pair of black lounge pants and a white t-shirt. The thin, cotton linen barely contained his large muscular arms and chest, and she could see a solid sleeve of tattoos as well as colorful artwork peeking out along the V-neck of his t-shirt. His thighs appeared even more broad and defined, and he had no socks on his tanned feet. Even standing in casual clothes, Nikolai still appeared dangerous and sexy as hell. She could feel the heat coming off him and warming her skin as his eyes roamed over her body. Needing space before she did something stupid, Piper put distance between them before she started folding her clothes and putting them away.

"I just wanted to check on you and see how you're doing. Is the room satisfactory?"

"Um, yeah." Piper chuckled lightly at the absurdity of his question. "You know I could have hunkered down at the Best Western down the road. I really didn't need a room that cost as much as this one."

"Are you complaining?" Nikolai asked, unable to read her yet. "If you don't like the room, I'm sure we can find another hotel in the morning."

"No, I'm not complaining. This place is amazing! I'm sorry, I was just being sarcastic, and you don't deserve that. I really do appreciate everything you have done for me tonight. I can cut you a check for the rooms and your airfare tomorrow morning."

"That won't be necessary. Consider yourself my guest."

"Thanks." She smiled softly, unnerved at the way he stared at her. "Look, I wanted to ask you something. I have clinicals in about 4 hours and was hoping to be able to go. Think that can be arranged?"

"I'm sorry but I can't let you do that."

"Why? This is my first year of med school and it's really important that I don't miss class. I..."

He silenced her words by stepping closer to her. Lifting her chin with his fingers he gently said. "My refusal for you to go isn't personal Piper. Grecoff and Paul will know in a couple hours that you have accessed the money if they don't already. Once they do, they will want you dead. They can easily find out where you attend school or places that you frequent. Unfortunately, until we take out the threat they pose, you will have to stay here."

She felt her body begin to shake uncontrollably as the heat from Nikolai's fingertips slowly traced her jawline. She didn't like his response, but she also didn't have a death wish. Clearing her throat, she found herself wanting to rub her face against the palm of his hand. Pulling back and pushing aside Nikolai's hand she said softly. "That's kind of what I thought you'd say. I don't really like it, but I get it. Are you okay with me emailing my professor and doing some stuff online?"

"Of course. If you think it would help you any, I would be glad to email your professor as well. Maybe my attorney, Artem, could pull together some type of document that will help you with your absence. There are probably only so many days you can miss?"

"Yeah. I appreciate you doing that for me. While we are talking about emailing school, what about my cellphone? I would like to have it back so I can talk to Andy when I want."

"Sure, that can be arranged. However, she will be your only point of contact verbally." Nikolai smiled, loving the way her eyes touched his. He could see the sincere appreciation in her dazzling blue eyes. "So, if you don't mind me asking, what is your plan with medical school? Do you want to specialize?"

"I want to do surgery on the brain and spinal cord."

"A neurosurgeon huh? Ambitious. You want to make the big bucks huh?"

A soft smile touched Piper's lips as she chuckled. "Something like that. I have just always found the human brain fascinating. No offense but I'm surprised you knew what my specialty would be called."

"Well believe it or not Ms. Williamson, I actually considered med school myself at one time." The grey-eyed giant smiled, her soft laughter infectious as she pulled out her clothes from her bag and folded them.

Her eyes immediately met his as she asked in surprise, "Really? What changed your mind?"

"My brother Zan actually." He replied, thinking of the man he had talked to just moments ago.

"He didn't approve of you going to med school?" She questioned, curious to learn more about him as she sat down on the bed. Pulling herself back some, she crossed her legs Indian style. "Was it due to financial reasons or have you always had money?"

Sitting on the edge of the bed himself, the large man countered. "It had nothing to do with finances sweetheart and my brother was completely on board with me becoming a doctor. I say Zan changed my mind, but it was nothing he did directly. I knew I wanted to either be a trauma surgeon or go into business for myself. When I realized the time and commitment it would take for med school, I decided on business. Knowing who and what my family is, I didn't want all of that responsibility falling on my brother's shoulders, and it would have if I had chosen the medical path. He would hate me telling you this but Zan was pissed when he found out I changed majors, but he got over it in time. Plus, I'm not ashamed to admit that I saw a friend of mine get shot in the chest as a young adult and the sight made me ill. Not sure if I had a strong enough stomach to do surgery in the long run."

"You shouldn't feel shame in that. The sight of blood definitely takes some getting used to. The first time I had to sew up a cut on a guy's arm, I thought I was going to pass out, but I fought through it and did quite well." Piper smiled, tucking a strand of hair behind her ear. "So, this family business you talk about. Is it just you and your brother?"

"Da." Nikolai responded, shaking his head. "Zan and I both have legit businesses and then we have family business. The legit side of business deals with gas and oil."

"And the family business?"

"Is a conversation we can save for another time." Seeing the questions in her furrowed brow, he grinned. "It's not that I don't want to answer your questions, it's just complicated. We have a few days together so we can dive into it once you've had some sleep."

"Oh." Piper remarked as she cast her eyes down. Seeing her hand only inches from his, she reached over and covered it with hers. When her eyes met his again, the breath caught in her throat at the intense lust she saw there. Her pulse quickened and she stumbled over her words. "I, just um, want to say, um, thank you...for everything. There has got to be some way I can repay you for your kindness Nikolai. I'm sure you would rather be at home with Mrs. Volkov and the kids than here with me."

Interlocking his fingers with hers, he brought the back of her hand to his lips. "There is no Mrs. Volkov back in Russia nor are their children." Leaning closer to her, his lips hovered over hers as he said in a deep, husky voice. "However, know this sweetheart. When I'm ready for some type of repayment, you'll be the first to know."

The breath caught in her throat when his clean-shaven face seductively rubbed against her cheek instead of kissing her. She felt the moan escape her lips when his free hand slid up her left calf and thigh. Just as her hand trailed up his muscular forearm to the massive bicep, Piper's lips found Nikolai's jaw. However, just as her lips tasted the skin there, he jerked away from her as if he had been shot and jumped to his feet. She then watched in a mixture of lust and confusion as the bratva leader put space between them, coming to stand in the doorway of the room.

"I'm sorry about that. I don't want you to think I am trying to take advantage of you. Why don't you go ahead and try to get some rest? As you know it's super late. Why don't you send your emails and then try to sleep?" Nikolai asked, clearing his throat and trying to calm his boiling blood. She had been so soft and responsive to his touch. He would swear he saw desire light her blue eyes. This woman was too dangerous to his senses. He needed to make sure he kept his distance from her.

"Yeah…yeah. That's a good idea." Piper replied, her body on fire being so close to him. He smelled so good, and his body was so warm. She wanted to wrap herself around Nikolai and feel every inch of him snuggled against her. She had always been able to control herself with men, but she could not seem to be able with him. "Again, thank you for everything tonight. You have no idea how much you have changed my life already."

"Any plans on what you are going to buy first with all that cash?"

"No idea actually. Maybe a vacation of sorts and then I'll probably put the rest toward school. I've never had money so the whole concept is foreign to me." Piper said, wrapping her arms around herself. "At the apartment, when I said I wanted Andy to have half of the money, I meant it. Can you help me make that happen?"

"Of course. We can talk about it after breakfast tomorrow if you want. Listen if you need anything tonight, just yell. I'm a pretty light sleeper so I'm sure I will be able to hear you. If for some reason I don't, Mikhas is right across the hall." He stated genuinely, his pulse flexing in his jaw as he leaned against the door frame. Why was it so damn hard for him to walk away from her? Seeing her, sitting there in the bed, had him wanting to lay her back slowly and devour her lips.

"I shouldn't need anything. I'm really tired so…"

"Good night." And with that Nikolai was gone.

Piper fell over on the bed and immediately buried her face in a pillow as she screamed into it. She couldn't believe that she had almost kissed him again! She was furious at herself for acting like a trollop in heat. *This guy is dangerous and with the mafia* she reminded herself, *not your future boyfriend*! She was simply going to blame her behavior with him on fatigue, liquor, and a lack of sleep. It had also been almost a year since she had sex last. He was handsome and ridiculously attractive, but she was not that hard up. No way in hell she was going to sleep with a criminal, especially one who had her locked up in a suite. As she lay there and thought about the distance she was going to keep between herself and Nikolai, her eyes began to flutter and in seconds, Piper was fast asleep.

Chapter 6

Piper sat in her bedroom attempting to finish a report for school. She had spent the last thirty minutes on the same paragraph and just couldn't seem to get her brain to focus on school and not on Nikolai Volkov. She had not seen the mountainous Russian in almost eighteen hours, even though she had intentionally looked for him. She had slept little this morning and was tired as hell. Piper thought talking to Andy this morning would help her stress, but her stepsister had been so panicked that it had only raised her own anxiety higher. With a loud sigh, she rolled her eyes and closed her laptop. Pushing it aside on her bed, the platinum blonde rubbed her stomach as it growled. Although it was almost nine pm, she was in the mood for a snack. After all, she had not eaten dinner and had worked out in the villa's gym for almost two hours that morning. She had seen someone stocking the refrigerator with food earlier, so maybe she could find something to take her mind off Nikolai and fill her belly.

Walking into the kitchen, Piper thought about her current situation. She had spent most of the day going over schoolwork and her sudden financial windfall. The bratva leader was right; the money was hers and she had full access to it. Although she had not seen Nikolai, she had done a virtual session with his personal accountant to help her plan what to do with the money. After paying off what few bills she had and giving Andy her half of the money, Piper had divided the rest up in a variety of secured accounts. The accountant had been so kind to her and had explained everything that was being done. Not only had he done that for her, but she had also been able to include Andy in the virtual meeting as well. Her step-sister had protested loudly and quite vocally to taking half of the money, but in the end, she had been left with no option but to take it. It was the least Piper could do to repay her for helping her out as a child and as an adult. She, herself, could still not get over that she was worth over a quarter of a billion dollars, but she was and had no idea what to do with that much money.

The thought of her new, sudden income had Piper thinking about her family again. The anger she felt in the pit of her stomach toward her grandfather was turning sour quickly. What kind of man allowed his only daughter to live in squalor and filth all those years? She had no idea if James had attempted to help her mother or not, but regardless, how could one not help an innocent child? Her grandfather knew that she existed and was living with a drug-addicted mother who resorted to prostitution for her drugs. Why didn't he ever attempt to reach out to her? It sounded as though Paul had at least grown up with money. Piper knew it took more than that to survive, but it was a hell of a lot more than she ever had. Her heart ached with the knowledge of having grandparents who had been missing from her life. Not only had they been missing, but they also knew how she was living and still had not cared. Even now, Piper had no idea why James had left her his money. Part of her wanted it, and part of her didn't. Yes, it would change her life entirely, but at what cost?

Hearing a sound behind her, she swung around to see Nikolai standing there. He was casually dressed in a pair of torn jeans and a grey, Henley style shirt. He had the long sleeves pushed up on his wide forearms and his hair was disheveled. Nikolai also had a day's growth of dark hair on his handsome, rugged face and looked as though he had not slept. Clearing her throat and meeting his eyes, she said in a soft, feminine voice, "I'm sorry if I disturbed you in any way. I was hungry and thought I'd get a snack. I'll be out of your way soon."

"You're not in my way, little one. I was feeling hungry myself." he replied, his voice deep and sexy. He had been unprepared for the sudden jolt to his system upon seeing her. Piper stood before him in a simple navy blue, knee length dress and her hair was pulled up in a loose bun. On her flaw-less face, she wore a pair of cute glasses that gave her an inno-cent, librarian appearance. He felt his semi-hard cock slightly pressing against the zipper of his jeans and closed his eyes. Nikolai had intentionally stayed away from her today because he had been able to think of nothing else since meeting her. The couple hours of sleep he had gotten had been full of erotic dreams, so he had opted to get up and work instead. Not only had he spent time on his own business, but Aleksandr had let him know that Paul and Grecoff knew about Piper having the money and that they had disappeared. Nikolai knew they were in hiding but would be back to Las Vegas soon.

"Since I was going to make myself some grub, would you like something as well?" Piper offered, her body igniting into flames as his eyes traveled her body. She pressed her legs together uncomfortably at the way he hungrily licked his lips when his gaze lingered on her legs and bottom. When his eyes met hers again, she asked, "What would you like?"

"Unfortunately, I can't have what I really want right now,"

Nikolai said huskily, stepping closer to her before shaking himself mentally and moving back. At the confused look on her face, he asked, "How about we order some room service? Care to join me for a snack?"

"Sure, that would be great."

Almost an hour later, the two sat in the game room at a small table, eating and laughing. Nikolai found himself completely enamored with his exquisite guest. Her voice and laugher were soft, raspy, and melodic, and he loved the small gap between her teeth. The more comfortable she became with him, the more she caressed his hand or stroked his arm without thought. He was finding that Piper was not only beautiful, but intelligent, sensitive, funny, and compassionate. Given the life she had been forced to live, she appeared quite well adjusted and positive about her future.

Watching her shoving a big bite of burger into her mouth, he chuckled. "I take it you are enjoying your meal."

"That obvious, huh?" She smiled, wiping her mouth before taking a drink of her wine. "It may not look like it but I'm a total junk food junkie. Or as Andy says, a connoisseur of comfort."

"What would you say is your favorite food?"

"Oh, wow. Now that's a loaded question." She laughed, loving Nikolai's easy smile. "First and foremost, I love a big, greasy burger. Then I would say it's a toss-up between pizza and French fries. However, if we are talking snacks only, then hands down, it would be Oreos."

"What is an Oreo?" the grey-eyed giant asked, loving her enthusiasm for food. It was refreshing to talk to someone who loved food as much as he did. When she grabbed her chest in mock horror and her eyes widened in shock, he grinned. "I'm sorry, did I ask the wrong question?"

"Are you really from this planet?" Piper exclaimed laughingly. "You don't know what an Oreo is? How do you not know what an Oreo is? I'm sorry, but I don't think we can be friends any longer, Mr. Volkov."

"I'm wounded, sweetheart. I'm sorry, but we don't have Oreos in my country. It must be an American snack? Care explaining what it is?"

"It's only the sweetest, most amazing cookie in the world and I am absolutely addicted to them!" she moaned fondly with a smile. Touching Nikolai affectionately on the arm, she added, "Okay, now let me educate you on one of the greatest American treats. It is two, thin chocolate wafers held together by a delicious, white confectioner's cream. They come in a pack and there are multiple flavors, however, my favorite is the Double Stuff. I eat them daily and wish I could have one now."

"Well, your enthusiasm for this cookie has me intrigued. I say we have someone pick some up for dessert." The dark-haired billionaire smiled, stifling a moan at the way Piper licked her plump, full lips. Damn, this woman was sexy even when thinking about food! Taking out his phone, he dialed a familiar number. When someone on the other end answered, he said, "My guest would like some Oreo cookies brought up."

Watching Nikolai hang up the phone, Piper laughed as she happily clapped her hands together. "Oh my gosh! Get ready for the best treat of your life."

"I can't wait. I think you are more excited about these cookies than you were the money you inherited."

"Yeah, well," she began dryly, rolling her eyes. "At least I know where the cookie comes from. I have no idea who has had their hands on the money."

"From what we found, your grandfather acquired the money honestly. It would appear as if he was a hard-working man. He came from nothing and worked his way to the top."

"Well, that makes me feel better, I guess," she replied, taking another drink of her wine before she stood up and walked over to the couch. Sitting down Indian style, she shrugged. "I think I would have rather had the relationship with him instead of the money, but he clearly didn't want that."

Grabbing his glass of wine, he joined her on the couch. He hated the sadness he saw in her eyes. Reaching out to stroke her cheek with his thumb, he said in a gentle voice, "I know all this has been hard for you, sweetheart. I don't understand your grandfather's actions, either, but maybe his intentions were different than they appear. It will be up to you to sort out how you feel about all of this. I wish I could make it easier for you, love. I'm not going to pretend to know how you feel. I do know that I would not have abandoned my daughter or my grandchild."

"Neither would I," Piper returned softly, meeting his eyes. She could feel the unshed tears burning the back of hers as they stared at each other. Refusing to cry in front of him, she grabbed the hand that stroked her jaw and held it affectionately. "Anyway, enough about me and my problems. Tell me about your folks. I know you said they were murdered. Were you close to them?"

"I was." He smiled, thinking of his mother and father fondly. "I have a handful of memories of my mother and father, however, I was so young when they were killed, I'm not sure if they are my true memories or ones that Zan has supplied me with. I do remember how affectionate they were with us and being snuggled by them both. They were not only affectionate with us, but they were always hugging and kissing each other. I don't think you could have found two people more in love. We have journals that belonged to my father, and in them, he frequently commented that his life didn't begin until he met Mama."

"That sounds beautiful. I'll bet it was quite lovely to witness firsthand. Unfortunately, love in my house was getting your spouse a beer or demonstrating your love for others with your fists. Hell, for my birthday one year, I got a pack of gum and a candy bar. However, Maury ended up eating both on a drunken bender before popping me across the face just because." When she saw his face soften with empathy and felt his hand begin rubbing her side in support and consolation, Piper shrugged off his actions and cleared her throat awkwardly. She had never told anyone that story, but somehow, Nikolai made her feel comfortable and... safe. "Look, just ignore that last part. I don't know why I even told you that. I don't need pity from anyone. Not everyone grows up living the American dream. Anyway, it would be nice if a love that sweet would find me, but I'm not going to hold my breath. Believe it or not, you are the first decent man I have met, or at least you seem to be."

Nikolai wanted to push her further but also didn't want to ruin the moment between them. Piper clearly was uncomfortable discussing her past and he doubted that she ever really did so. Wanting to keep her talking, he asked, "You don't believe in love?"

"Um, I don't know," she said honestly. "It's hard to believe in something you've never seen. I do like to pretend it is and happen to love the old black and white romance films. What about you? Do you believe in love? I can't imagine a man as handsome as yourself not having a harem of women following him around. I know you said you're not married, but is there a girlfriend or mistress back in Russia?"

"There is no girlfriend, but I do have a handful of women whom I see on a regular basis. I think you Americans call it friends with benefits, but I call them my submissives. As for do I believe in love, absolutely. I have not experienced it myself yet, but like I said, I've seen it in all its glory."

Piper hated the sudden feeling of disappointment filling her chest. Of course, this handsome man in front of her had several women. What had he called them? Submissives? She wondered if he was one of those BDSM Doms who tied women down and did the spanking thing. A couple of her friends were into that stuff, but she didn't find it appealing in the least. Growing up the way she did, with little to no control of her environment, it was difficult for her to even think about giving that to someone else, let alone sexually. She knew that men who were as wealthy and powerful as Nikolai typically engaged in activities like that. She couldn't deny her attraction to the Russian or that it had started in her apartment, so it only made sense that other women would be attracted to him too. However, why did the thought of this man being intimate with another woman make her chest ache painfully? She felt physically ill picturing him having sex with someone else. Piper didn't know this guy from Adam, but here she was already feeling jealous and possessive. She felt as though he was attracted to her too, but he had already rejected two advances on her part. Maybe she wasn't his type? Maybe he was keeping things professional? Either way, it was probably for the best. She had horrible luck with men and relationships, and the fact that she was attracted to Nikolai should be her first warning sign.

"So, what about you?" he asked, curious as to why she was suddenly so quiet. He could not read the expression on her face but could tell she was deep in thought. "Is there someone significant in your life?"

"Lord, no!" the blue-eyed woman exclaimed, pulling her hands back from his and crossing her arms over her chest. "I haven't had much luck with men in the past, so I choose to keep them at a distance right now. Maybe when I'm done with med school, I can focus on dating. You mentioned that you have submissives, are you a dominant?"

"Da, but by the look on your face, you appear disgusted with that. What do you think a dominant does?"

"Honestly?" she asked sarcastically as he shook his head. "I think men enjoy that lifestyle because it allows them to sleep with multiple women and control them. It's all about your pleasure anyway, right? Her needs aren't important in those types of relationships. Am I warm?"

"No, quite the opposite. I'm not sure who you personally know who has engaged in the lifestyle, but it is misrepresented by many who practice it, and to outsiders, it seems deviant or weird. However, nothing is further from the truth. As a dominant in the world of BDSM, my relationships are always consensual, and the woman can stop the love play at any time she likes simply by saying her safe word. It's about trust, little one, and quite frankly the most intimate, nurturing form of human contact. It can be very freeing, Piper. I would think you would be a little more open-minded."

She sat there and listened intently as Nikolai spoke. Although she was still not sure of what to think about BDSM, she could tell that he was telling her the truth, or at least he believed he was. The way he described it was very appealing, but Piper knew she would have serious issues with getting past the trust thing. She would be the first to admit that having this grey-eyed mountain dominate her sexually made every inch of her body tingle and her pussy weep with excitement. Even now, she wanted to lean forward and run her tongue along his lips and beg him to take her. Somehow, she knew that Nikolai would be a very giving and thoughtful lover, based on how he had treated her in the past twenty-four hours. His kindness toward her was one of the things that drew her to him, which wasn't good in her current situation.

Shaking herself, she broke eye contact as she quietly said, "Maybe I got the BDSM thing wrong. The couple of women I know who live the lifestyle have made it sound like it's all about sex and their dominants' whims. The men in control are jerks too. If I'm wrong, I'm wrong. I have no problems admitting that. Oh, and I am open-minded, Mr. Volkov."

Tipping his glass of wine to her, he said in a low, husky voice as his hand traveled up her leg to grip her knee, "Well, if you are ever interested in trying it, love, you just let me know." He groaned inwardly when her hand found his thigh and she leaned forward to kiss his lips. With a low growl, Nikolai hopped up off the couch to keep himself from devouring her. Walking to the table, he said over his shoulder, "Let me get us some more wine."

"Yeah, do that." She sighed, glad that he had stopped the interaction before she kissed him.

As he came back over and refilled their glasses, Nikolai asked, "Now you say that in the past, you have been unlucky regarding relationships with men. Why do you think that is?"

"I'm my own worst enemy sometimes," she replied honestly as she took a sip of her wine. "Let me just say this. If there was a room full of a hundred men and only one of them was a loser, I would pick him. I have no idea what that is about, but I wish it wasn't true. Men just typically treat me like an object, and I don't like it."

The grey-eyed man knew by the tone of her voice and shifting of her body posture that Piper didn't want to go into her personal life, at least regarding relationships. Nikolai hated the way she attempted to control the conversation and him with her words and actions. He'd be damned if he allowed her to continue doing that. Just to see what she would do, he asked, "Then why be an exotic dancer, love?"

"Know about that, do you? Of course, you do. Guess it was in my file," Piper remarked caustically, rolling her eyes. Suddenly feeling defensive, her body stiffened as she barked, "Look, I'm not some whore off the street who sells her body or gets off on men pawing her body for cash. I needed the money at the time, and it paid well. I'm not proud of the things I have done to survive, but I won't sit here and be judged by you or anyone."

"Put away the fucking claws, little one. You're the one jumping to conclusions, not me." Nikolai warned in an icy, cold voice as he gripped her throat loosely and brought her face abruptly to his. "We were having a nice conversation and I simply asked you a question. People who are trying to get to know each other do that. I wasn't judging you."

"I'm sorry," she whispered breathlessly, her pulse beating wildly as she held his intense gaze. His lips hovered above hers and she could smell the sweet scent of mint and wine on his breath. She heard him growl seconds before he shot to his feet and began pacing the area in front of her. Without looking at him, she said softly, "I didn't mean to upset you, Nikolai. Please don't be angry. I'm just so used to people assuming I'm a whore because of what I do. I don't even take my clothes off when I dance, but people make assumptions and spread lies."

"I'm not angry with you." He sighed gently as he walked back over to where she sat and began lightly stroking her cheek. When she began rubbing her face against the palm of his hand, he said, "I have no problems with you being a dancer, sweetheart. What a consenting adult does behind closed doors, is their business. I also understand that some-times in life, we do things that we don't necessarily want to do to survive. I've done them myself."

Feeling emotionally overwhelmed suddenly, Piper felt tears burning the back of her blue eyes. The sincerity she saw on his face was almost more than she could take. She had never had someone be so honest and compassionate with her before. Needing to touch him, she stood up on her tiptoes and threw her arms around his neck. Just as she pressed her breasts to his chest and brought his mouth down for a kiss, the sound of someone clearing a throat, had the couple releasing each other. Her embarrassment of being caught with the billionaire quickly turned into joy when she saw the pack of Oreos sitting nearby. When Nikolai attempted to grab the package of cookies, she smacked his hand and waved her index finger in front of him.

"I thought you were going to share," he asked with a deep chuckle. "Aren't these supposed to be amazingly good?"

"Oh, they are, but there is an art to eating them. Watch and learn." Piper grinned, pulling him down beside her on the couch. Pulling out a cookie and twisting one of the chocolate wafers off, she licked the creamy white center. "After you pull apart the cookie, you have to lick the middle of it. The cream is the best part. After you lick off the white goodness, then you pop it in your mouth and enjoy the taste of the best cookie ever."

The bratva leader could not respond as the pulse ticked wildly in his jaw. His semi-hard cock had twitched to life when her tongue had tasted the sweet filling. When she had moaned in pleasure at eating the treat, Nikolai had wanted to jerk her over his lap and bury himself inside her. Her giggles and moans were burning a path up his spine. What the hell was he going to do over the next few days, with this enticing creature within arm's reach? How was he going to cope? He wanted this woman with every fiber in his being and was having a difficult time keeping his hands off her.

"Now it's your turn. Here, I'll feed you the first one." She smiled, getting on her knees beside him on the couch. She pulled out another cookie and twisted the wafer, exposing the filling. The breath once again caught in her throat when her eyes met Nikolai's intense, heated gaze. Man, this guy was magnificent, and he was looking at her as if she were his next meal. Was that sexual tension she felt blasting every inch of exposed skin? Did he want her as much as she wanted him? With a breathy, shaky voice, she huskily said, "Have a taste and tell me what you think."

A low, animalistic growl escaped his lips as he pushed the cookie away, gripped her face in his hands, and captured her mouth in a fiery, passionate kiss. As his hands found their way down her body, Nikolai had her straddle his lap and mated his tongue with hers. The moan caught in his throat when she aggressively pushed her hands under his t-shirt and massaged his hairless, muscular chest. His cock slammed against the zipper of his pants and his body erupted in flames as Piper began to undulate herself against him. Fuck, this woman was driving him insane! How could he be respectful to her when all he wanted to do was dominate her?

"Piper," he growled, gripping her neck loosely and pushing her back. He stifled a groan when he saw the desire and lust darkening her eyes. "We need to stop."

"Why?" she asked shakily, circling her hips against his groin. She could feel how much he wanted her by the large erection in his jeans. Why the hell would he want to stop? Her clitoris was throbbing painfully, and her core was dripping with its own wet excitement. She gasped when he suddenly stopped her hips. She was almost suffocated with disappointment immediately and lowered her head to whisper, "Don't you want me, Nikolai? I want you."

"You don't feel that, sweetheart?" Nikolai asked huskily, raising his hips so she could feel the bulge between his legs. Lifting her chin with his finger, he said, "Of course, I want you but I'm trying to be sensitive to you right now. I think we should wait to have sex after I take care of your little problem."

"But I don't want to wait," she quickly replied, her hands roaming over his chest and rippled abdomen. When she felt his hands slide under her dress to begin massaging her bottom, she leaned forward to run her tongue seductively along his bottom lip. "And I don't think you do, either. Why can't we just enjoy each other's company while we're together?"

"We can, but that complicates things. Are you ready for that?" Nikolai questioned, studying her eyes as they stared into his. He could see a broad range of emotions there.

"I'm ready for you," she answered honestly, nuzzling his neck. Piper almost purred when his finger slid in her panties and traced her pussy lips. Pulling at his earlobe with her teeth, she whispered in his ear, "I'm not expecting a commitment from you, just sex. I'm attracted to you, and you are attracted to me. You said yourself, you have friends with benefits. Think of me as that."

The large Russian snarled as he slammed his mouth against hers before he jerked her dress up over her head. His fingers quickly got rid of her bra before his mouth found her puffy, plump breasts. Nikolai squeezed the globes together before plucking at her nipples with his teeth. When she arched her back to give his hot, wet mouth more freedom, he roughly slapped one ass cheek before he flipped her over on the couch and lay between her open thighs. He felt her fingers dig into his hair and pull his mouth down for a kiss as he ground his clothed erection against her pussy. As he broke the kiss, he locked her hands above her head to still her movements, but her shapely legs wrapped around his waist instead.

"I want to touch you," she heard herself say in a soft, pleading voice. She could not believe how wanton she was being or how aggressive he was. She was used to controlling sex, not being controlled. However, something about the way he did it, excited her greatly.

"Let's get one thing straight, sweetness," Nikolai growled near her ear as his mouth seared a path across her jaw. "I know you like being in control, but not this time. I'm the dominant one in this relationship, not you. I give the orders, and you take them. Think you can handle that?"

"I think so," she breathlessly replied. The desire and lust she felt was burning her alive, but she couldn't stop the sudden wave of nervousness that dampened her passion slightly. She had never allowed a man to dominate her before. Piper liked calling the shots because that kept her from getting emotionally involved or physically hurt. However, Nikolai was somehow different. She felt things for him that she had never felt before. She knew there were different types of dominants, but what type was he? What if she didn't like what he was doing? "Will you stop if I don't like it?" she asked softly.

"Of course. Have you ever used a safe word?" Nikolai queried, placing a soft kiss on her neck. The vulnerability he saw in her blue eyes had him wanting to fiercely protect her. When she shook her head in response to his question, he said, "Well then, we have to come up with one. A safe word stops everything in its tracks. If you feel uncomfortable at any time, just say firefly. Now what's your safe word?"

"Firefly," she barely whispered against his lips before her mouth was devoured by his. The blue-eyed beauty moaned in ecstasy when he released her hands and broke the kiss to trail a path down her neck, shoulders, and chest. When his hot tongue began lapping at one rose-colored nipple, his long, slender fingers began to manipulate her clit. Piper arched her back and ground her hips against his hand as his teeth playfully pulled at her breasts. She then felt his mouth move lower down her stomach and between her thighs. Her pussy wept with passion when Nikolai placed kisses on her inner thighs before sitting back on his heels.

Tearing off his t-shirt and tossing it on the floor, he stared down at her flawless body. He licked his lips hungrily as his eyes devoured every inch of her. Her body was the epitome of femininity and perfection. Her curly, platinum hair hung in wild disarray over her breasts as she stared at him with hooded, lust-filled eyes. He sat between curvy, wide hips that met at the apex of her womanhood. Her pussy had a thin strip of blonde hair and glistened with her essence. Nikolai's mouth watered and his throat went dry at the thought of tasting her. He absently rubbed his rock-hard, throbbing cock through his pants and moaned. His body was fully engulfed in flames and this little American was the only thing that could extinguish the fire.

As Nikolai undid his pants, he was surprised to feel her small, warm hands slide into the zipper and begin rubbing the silky skin of his cock. He immediately jerked her hands away and again locked them above her head. When she began wiggling against him in protest, he nibbled a path up her jaw to her ear. At her ear, he growled, "I told you, I am the dominant and you are the submissive. You can touch me when I say you can. Since you can't appear to listen or obey the rules, I need to bind your hands."

The voluptuous blonde's breathing was sharp and shallow as she watched him grab his t-shirt from the floor and quickly bind her hands. Her eyes then hungrily feasted on his amazing, well-defined body when he rested back on his heels and removed his thick, veiny cock from the confines of his pants. She felt the moisture from her pussy pooling under her bottom as Nikolai began to stroke the length slowly and deliberately, with long, unhurried motions. Her head fell back when he circled the mushroom-shaped head around her engorged clit before sliding it up and down the open slit. As he thumped his cock against her vaginal lips, Piper knitted her brow in frustration as she tried to move her hips to capture it deep in her core. She cried out in a mixture of pain and frustration when his hand smacked her mound.

"Firefly!" Piper gasped breathlessly as she undulated uncomfortably against the hand tracing the soaking wet skin of her core. "No hitting, okay? I just want you inside me."

Nikolai slid two fingers inside her pussy and began moving them in and out as he leaned over her and placed a gentle kiss on her lips. "Patience, sweet one," he said huskily, a seductive smile playing on his lips. "You are going to feel every inch of me inside you but first, I want to taste that beautiful cunt. Do you want me to taste you?"

"Yes," she said breathlessly against his lips as he rubbed his cheek against hers, then blazed a trail of kisses down her neck, chest, and stomach again before positioning himself between her legs.

Nikolai watched her glistening pussy contract and pulse as he spread the lips with his fingers. Her body was amazing to look at! Never in his life, had he wanted a woman as much as he wanted this one. It was taking every ounce of his self-control to go slow, but something deep inside told him that she needed him to. Leaning forward, he ran his tongue up over the engorged, sensitive nub. A shiver ran through him when he tasted her sweet essence. Damn, this woman tasted like warm honey. A chuckle escaped his mouth when his tongue found the spot again and Piper cried out in ecstasy. He could not get over how responsive she was to his gentle caresses. He wanted to plunge inside her warmth but also wanted to give her great pleasure, and by the sound of her moans, he was doing just that.

Piper arched her back as the dark-haired giant devoured her hard little nub and quickened the pace of the fingers moving in and out of her core. She undulated her pussy against his mouth and her fingers gripped his black hair as the pressure of her impending orgasm grew. She had never really enjoyed oral sex with men and had been bored the couple of times she had done it, but Nikolai's mouth felt like heaven. Piper loved the way his tongue lapped at the sensitive spot and the way he brought her closer and closer to the edge, only to pull back to nibble on the lips. When he sucked her clit back into his mouth and added a third digit into the play, she screamed out as the powerful orgasm tore her body into a million pieces. Her hips writhed and squirmed against his face, but instead of pulling back, Nikolai pressed her core even closer to his mouth to drink every drop of her essence. As the extraordinary sensation began to subside and her soul began to float back down to her body, Piper felt him place a kiss on the inside of each thigh and slowly caress his way up her torso with his masculine face.

"How was that?" he asked huskily, licking his lips and loving the taste of her. "Did my mouth feel good?"

"That was amazing," she countered, euphoric and breathless, bringing her bound hands over his neck. "Will you please untie my hands? I want to touch you."

"Yes, but you need to do something for me," he returned with a wicked smile on his face. After untying her hands, he positioned his cock at the entrance of her core and eased the fat, mushroom-shaped head inside. They both moaned in unison before he said, "Tell me what you need, baby. If you want me inside you, then say 'fuck me, sir'."

The blue-eyed belle wanted this man desperately, but her pride wouldn't allow her to beg. When she did not respond to his command, Nikolai pulled out from her wet warmth and began to slowly stroke his cock. She watched the sweat glisten off his muscular chest and the precum ooze from the head of his thick, heavy rod. When he went to stand up, she sat up quickly and tried to grab at his arm. "Where are you going?" she asked, suddenly feeling a chill without him being close. "You can't leave yet. We haven't had sex."

"And we won't unless I hear you say the words."

She quickly went around his big body. Catching him off guard, she was able to push him, so he fell back on the couch. She straddled his hips and tried to capture his lips with hers, but Nikolai loosely gripped her neck and stopped her actions. With ease, he flipped her over on his lap, so she lay on her stomach across his knees. Before she could utter a sound, his hand came down painfully on one bare cheek. Piper cried out and wiggled on his lap before she immediately stilled her movements and said in a soft whisper, "Firefly."

Nikolai instantly swooped her up in his arms and cradled her in his lap. He gently stroked her face and placed a soft kiss on her lips. Lifting her chin, he searched her ocean blue eyes. "Did I hurt you? Why did you use your safe word?"

"I told you earlier, I don't want to do the spanking thing," Piper replied nervously in a barely audible voice. Although she had never been spanked and his actions had caught her off guard, she could not help the warm feeling of arousal spreading across her stomach and chest. Even now, her bottom stung from the blow of his hand, but her pussy was dripping with wetness. The reason she had said her safe word was because she was overcome with such raw, powerful emotions that she had momentarily felt suffocated.

He swore that he had seen desire light her eyes for a moment, but she was now shielding her feelings from him and he didn't like that. "I spanked your bottom because you refused to comply with my demands and then tried to aggressively top me. When my submissives intentionally break the rules, they are punished. Now answer my question. Did I physically hurt you with the spanking?"

"No, you didn't," she said truthfully as she straddled his lap. She couldn't tell what he was thinking or feeling and that worried her. She still desperately wanted this man inside her but couldn't tell if he felt the same. Wanting him to understand her, she threw her hands around his neck and played with the hair there. "The emotions were just too much. I—"

Nikolai captured her words in his mouth with a kiss. He knew exactly how she was feeling because he had almost come unglued when his hand connected with her ass. His cock had throbbed so painfully that the precum oozing from the large head had spilled onto her stomach. He hadn't anticipated such honesty from her, but he was glad he got it. The growl escaped the back of his throat when he broke the kiss and spread her ass cheeks wide with his hands. "Apology accepted, sweet one. Now tell me that you want me inside you. Say 'sir, fuck me hard'."

Swallowing the lump in her throat, she ran her tongue across his bottom lip as she looked deep into his dark grey eyes. "Sir, fuck me hard. I need you inside me."

"Good girl," the muscular mountain moaned into her mouth before he positioned her above his cock and slowly eased her down the length of it. His head fell back a moment in pure ecstasy at the tight, snug feeling he encountered as he stretched her vaginal walls wide. Man, this woman felt incredible. Reaching under her hips, he slid her back up his cock, only to drop her back down and bury himself inside her, balls deep. Nikolai hid the smile that threatened to touch his lips when Piper's eyes fluttered closed and she whimpered in delight. "Do I feel good inside you?"

"So good," Piper purred against his mouth as her dark-haired lover set up a delicious, steady rhythm. Capturing his lips with hers, their tongues mated as she rode him. She loved the friction his light chest hair was causing against her nipples and the way he caressed her clitoris with one hand. She then quickened the pace, following Nikolai's lead, bouncing up and down on his cock. As she rode him faster and with more gusto, she felt the pressure building between her legs. When she heard him urging her to come, Piper fully embedded him within her core and rocked back and forth at a frenzied pace. With one final undulation of her hips, her head fell back and the scream escaped her lips as she came hard on his thick cock. Her body exploded into a million pieces and her pelvic floor convulsed around him as she rode the enormous swell of rapture.

As her voluptuous body pulsed and thrashed against him, Nikolai could no longer stand the sweet torture she was causing him and he, too, exploded, deep within her pussy. Her wet, warm walls quivered and milked his cock of its essence as his lips tasted hers and he hugged her body tightly to his. He rode his own intense wave of pleasure at the luxurious feeling she had created inside him. He had never come so hard or so fast with a woman before and had always prided himself on control. But with Piper, he appeared to have none. Even now, his chest swelled with the oddest sensations at the way she cuddled against him and her breathing became steady.

The platinum blonde sighed in splendor as a quiet calm settled between the two of them and Nikolai's fingers traced her spine. The sex had been phenomenal but as the fog of the orgasm lifted, she began to think about what had occurred. The longer her lover held her, the more insecure she became. As she felt his cock receding inside her, Piper also realized that they had engaged in sex without a condom. Not only that, but she had been the aggressor! Hard telling what he thought of her and she wasn't going to stick around and find out.

"Look at me, love," he commanded as her eyes met his. "I would like to continue this in my bedroom. Will you stay with me tonight?"

"Um... I..." Piper began nervously, stumbling over her words. Her body yearned to be close to him, but her head told her to put on the brakes. "I'd better go to bed." She then slid off his cock and lap before she swooped up her discarded clothes and tried to cover herself. "Thanks for the burger and great sex. I guess I'll see you in the morning." She then turned and quickly left the room.

Chapter 7

Nikolai finished his morning call with Aleksandr as he clicked off the virtual meeting and sat back in his chair. His brother would be arriving in three days and so would Paul and Grecoff, at least according to their sources. The two men had discovered that the Volkov brothers had already intercepted the money and helped Piper to acquire it and they were pissed. Now, more than ever, they wanted her dead and had been able to procure several more men, with the promise of her fortune. To their advantage, this recruitment of men gave Aleksandr and Nikolai an opportunity to insert spies into the enemy's inner circle. Aleksandr was also sending more guards to Las Vegas for added protection, should there be any surprises. The younger Volkov had already talked with Mikhas and bumped up security around the hotel. Once the other guards arrived from Russia, he would strategically put them around the American woman. His main priority was to keep her safe and he would protect Piper at all costs.

Thinking of keeping the blonde safe had Nikolai's mind

instantly replaying their sexual encounter last night. He had not been able to sleep a wink and his body was still humming from being inside the beautiful medical student. He had wanted to spend the night with her but had anticipated her refusal. Nikolai had felt the change in her remarkable body and knew the moment she had gotten into her own head. When she had left the room, he had wanted to chase her and fuck her back into submission but had also wanted to foolishly prove to himself that he could keep his distance from her. Due to that stupidity, his night had been miserable, and he had quickly discovered that Piper had already seeped into his veins after their one encounter. He had found himself standing outside the door of her bedroom at one point, fighting for some semblance of control. Even now, he wanted to slip into her bed but wouldn't. *You're stronger than this, Nik*, he chided himself. *You are the one in control of your emotions, not her.*

Nikolai swore loudly as he jumped out of his chair and turned to look out the window of his suite. Laying his head against the cool glass, he closed his eyes a moment and breathed deeply. What the hell was wrong with him? He prided himself on having control of everything in his life, including his sexual relationships. As he told Piper last night, he did have sexual submissives who were his friends but not one of them had affected Nikolai the way the curvy blonde had. Everything about her had his body and senses heightened and overly sensitive. When he had spanked her last night, he had been overcome with strong feelings of protection, possession, and male dominance. Even though he had wanted to continue her punishment, he was glad that Piper had said her safe word because he, too, had been overcome with new, raw emotions. In fact, he couldn't wait to make her submit again. She clearly had issues with giving him control and externally wore her emotional scars, but she had let Nikolai know just how much she had wanted him. He had every intention of sleeping with her again but knew she would need to take it slow, even though she had been the aggressor last night.

"Hey, Nik, got a sec?" Mikhas asked, interrupting the grey-eyed giant's thoughts.

"Of course," Nikolai replied, turning around to look at his friend. "What's on your mind?"

"I just got off the phone with Vor and the additional men are in the air as we speak," Mikhas replied, referencing his best friend and head of Volkov security. "They should arrive sometime this evening."

"Thank you for the update. Oh, by the way, Chernoff is in Los Angeles on business and will be dropping by later this morning for a meeting. Make sure you notify the men that he is allowed up."

"Da, Pakhan," Mikhas said as he watched the younger man rub his tired, clean-shaven face. "You okay? You look a little tired this morning. Did everything go all right with Piper last night?"

"Not really," Nikolai said with a small smile. "I made the mistake of mixing business and pleasure last night. Against my better judgment, I might add."

"You don't make mistakes, Niki. Was it worth it, though?"

Nikolai chuckled at his friend's response as he looked at the brown-haired man. Licking his lips, he said honestly, "Yes, it was, actually. Maybe too worth it, to be exact. The hell of it is I intend on mixing them again. Tonight, as a matter of fact."

"Like I said, if you are going to do it again, then it wasn't a mistake," Mikhas said over his shoulder as he headed toward the door. He had sensed the sexual attraction between Nikolai and Piper from the moment they met and knew how last night had ended before he even asked. His boss's involvement with the woman would just make an already intriguing situation a little more interesting.

"Is Piper up yet?" the Russian asked before his lead guard left the room.

"Nyet. Do you want me to wake her?"

"No. Just notify me the moment she does wake up. Also order some breakfast for the men. I want to make sure everyone is eating."

"You got it," the guard returned before exiting the room.

Downstairs, she groaned and her eyes fluttered open before abruptly closing because of the light filtering into the room. She had been unable to sleep but had finally drifted off about two hours ago from exhaustion. Even then, her sexual encounter with Nikolai had plagued her dreams. She had silently cursed herself for leaving her dark-haired protector on the couch last night but had just been so overwhelmed with emotion that she would not allow herself the luxury of him. Every inch of her body had ached painfully without him nearby. Piper had never felt anything like this before and she didn't quite understand why she felt it with Nikolai. She had no idea what his true intentions were, but she felt safe and protected with him. He had been so kind to her and had treated her with respect, despite the situation. There was also a chemistry between the two of them that was so natural and explosive that it scared her. Sex with him had been ridiculously amazing and she still could not get past how aggressive she had been. She had never allowed a man to dominate her but with the bratva leader, it had felt right. *You're the one who complicated this shit*, she thought to herself. *Now what in the hell are you going to do?*

Sitting up in the bed, she was unprepared for the soreness she felt from her inner thighs and pussy. A soft smile, however, settled on her lips at how wide she had spread her legs to straddle him. Piper had barely got her legs wrapped around his waist but when she had, he had fit her body perfectly. His large, delicious cock had filled every inch of her core and had brought her unbelievable orgasms. She inwardly chastised herself for allowing such thoughts because all it did was make her want Nikolai that much more. Sex had always been okay with other men, but he had made her body explode with pleasure. She still could not get over the fact that she had enjoyed him slapping her bottom and dominating her. Although Piper had verbally protested quickly and said the safe word, she had not wanted him to stop. As she had honestly told him last night, she had been overwhelmed with feelings that were foreign to her and she got scared. Even now, the blue-eyed beauty's body craved Nikolai and she wanted to beg him to make love to her. Truth be told, she would do just that if she wasn't mortified about her actions. One minute, she was telling him how there was no way she would ever be a submissive and the next, she was allowing him to take what he wanted without question.

With a loud sigh, Piper rolled her neck before hopping out of bed. *You are going to be productive today, miss, and not think obsessively about Nikolai,* she told herself as she made her way to the bathroom. She quickly washed up and brushed her teeth before she pulled on a mauve colored sports bra and black leggings. After pulling her curly hair into a ponytail, she made her way out of the bedroom. However, before she made it to the gym, she stopped in the kitchen area to grab a drink. Just as she turned around with the water, Mikhas was standing in the doorway.

"Good morning Piper." The attractive man smiled as he

walked past her to pour himself a cup of coffee. "How are you this morning?"

"Peachy," she offered offhandedly as she downed some of the cold, clear liquid and headed toward the door. "Now if you'll excuse me."

"Where do you think you're headed this morning?" Mikhas said with a grin as she turned to glare at him. Just because he wanted to irritate her, he said, "I wasn't told that you had asked one of my men for permission to leave."

"Didn't realize I had to," she barked hotly, annoyed by his remark.

"Well, you do," he said, hiding his smile. This one had fire, just like Sophia. "Nikolai wants to know where you are at all times."

"And where is Nikolai this morning?" Piper asked, trying to hide the fact that she wanted to see him.

"In his office. Would you like for me to tell him that you want to speak to him?"

"No, I was just wondering," she quickly lied, before she turned to head back toward the door. Hearing Mikhas clear his throat before she crossed the threshold of the doorway, she stopped in her tracks and said over her shoulder, "I was going to work out. I would think that my outfit made that obvious, but I guess I was wrong."

Since Piper didn't turn around to deliver her annoyed remark, she didn't see the smile that touched his lips. "No, I realized where you were going but I still didn't hear you ask permission."

With an annoyed sigh, she turned around to look at him. With a false smile and insincere sweetness dripping from her words, she asked, "Mikhas, may I please go and work out this morning?"

"How long do you think you'll be? I will have to post a man outside the room so I can ensure your safety."

"I don't know. Like an hour?"

"That'll be fine," Mikhas said, tipping his coffee cup toward her before taking a sip. "Enjoy yourself."

An hour later, Piper climbed off the step mill and wiped the sweat from her face, neck, and chest. It had felt so good to release some of her emotions in the workout and now she was famished. Downing the rest of her water, she tossed it in the trash and knocked on the door. A huge, Viking of a man mumbled for her to follow him before she did as he instructed. Instead of leading her back to her portion of the suite, he walked her out on the balcony where Nikolai sat reading a newspaper. To his left, sat an elaborate, beautifully decorated table that was being set by staff. As soon as she stepped out into the warm sunlight, the Russian put down his paper and her body immediately shot up in flames as his grey eyes scanned her form. Before she knew what was happening, he was towering over her and crushing his body to hers before he devoured her lips. Her hands immediately slid into his ebony hair and began massaging his scalp as his tongue mated with hers. Just as his hands slid down her waist and began to jiggle and fondle her round, plump bottom, she heard someone clearing his throat behind them.

"I didn't mean to interrupt, sir," the servant began nervously as Nikolai broke the kiss to glare at him. "But I wanted to see if you would like for me to begin serving the food."

With a low growl, he kissed Piper's lips once more and pulled away. As he stepped over to pull out a chair for her to sit down, he said to the younger man, "Yes, that would be fine."

Taking her seat, she watched Nikolai take the chair across from her and the servant quickly fill her glass with juice. Her heart was beating wildly in her chest and her vaginal walls pulsed with need as her lover clenched his jaws and watched her closely. Damn, the intensity was rolling off him in waves this morning. He looked so handsome, dressed in a pair of khakis, a grey and white striped shirt, and a grey blazer, complete with a colorful pocket square. His face was clean-shaven and his hair immaculate. His eyes were devouring her and that made Piper excited but more so, nervous. She would swear she saw desire deep in their grey depths, but she wasn't sure. What if she was mistaking his anger for lust? Whatever he was feeling, she was about to find out.

***

Nikolai shifted uncomfortably in his chair as his cock throbbed against the zipper of his pants. Fuck, it was hard to control his emotions when this woman was nearby. As he took a seat and the servant prepared their plates, he fought for his emotions, saying, "I hope you haven't had breakfast yet. I thought we could eat together this morning."

"No, I haven't," Piper replied softly, rubbing her arm as she kept her eyes on the table. "I was going to wait until after my workout was finished."

"Good," he said, trying to read her body language. Why the hell was she suddenly so nervous? "I wasn't sure what you would like so I ordered one of everything on the menu."

"I'm pretty much a garbage disposal." She half smiled as her blue eyes finally found his. "I'll eat anything."

"So, will I." Nikolai grinned back as he waved off the hotel staff. He loved smelling her soft, sweet scent on the warm morning breeze. "Did you sleep well last night?"

"No, no, I didn't. Did you?"

"Nyet. Sleep escaped me last night. Someone was plaguing my thoughts."

Her eyes again met his. She loved the way they smoldered

as they stared at her. Without saying her name, Nikolai was letting her know that she was his plague. Piper licked her suddenly dry lips before she softly said, "Yeah, I know exactly what you mean." She then broke eye contact with him as she began eating her breakfast and an uncomfortable silence fell between them. Unable to maintain it, she blurted, "So why did you really want to eat breakfast with me this morning? I mean, you could have had food delivered to the suite and eaten upstairs. What's really going on?"

"Can't a man be nice?" Nikolai asked, wiping his mouth as her eyes again met his. "Maybe I just wanted to see you this morning, especially after you ended things so abruptly last night. However, aside from wanting to ask you a couple questions, I thought we could discuss new information I obtained on Paul and Grecoff."

"Paul and Grecoff? What about them? Have they realized the money is gone?" Piper asked, fear evident in her raspy voice.

"Don't be scared, sweetheart. You will be safe and protected," he reassured her as he reached across the table and looped his fingers with hers. "Paul and Grecoff have discovered the missing money and are now on their way back to Las Vegas. They have also recruited new men, but that mistake has allowed us to infiltrate their inner circle with spies. Not only will Paul and Grecoff grace us with their appearance in three days, but so will my brother and several additional guards."

"So, does that mean you are going to take them out here? Aren't you afraid of possibly getting caught murdering two men? What if something goes wrong?"

"Nothing will go wrong. I know it's hard for you to understand my lifestyle because the only way you've seen it portrayed is in the movies, but I can assure you, killing Paul and Grecoff will be done in a very discreet, secretive manner. My brother, myself, and our top guards are working out a plan as we speak. They are bringing the battle to us, sweetheart, and we plan on ending it. At no time, will you be put in danger. You have my word on that."

"But what about you, Nikolai?" Piper asked, swallowing the fear and anxiety that was a large lump in her throat as she squeezed his hand. "I don't want you to put yourself in danger, either. What if something happens to you?"

Standing up, he leaned across the table to place a gentle kiss on her lips. He rubbed his nose against hers softly and allowed himself to breathe in her feminine scent momentarily. Sitting back in the chair, he shook himself mentally before a light smile touched his face. "I appreciate you thinking of me, but nothing will happen to me, either, love. You have my word on that as well."

Feeling herself melting into Nikolai's grey eyes and touch, she jerked her hand away from his, cleared her throat, and started eating again. Avoiding his gaze, she said, "Well, I'm glad to hear that. I mean… you've been so nice to me and I would hate to see something happen to you. I appreciate you giving me the update. Will I need to do anything when Paul and Grecoff get here?"

The smile on the bratva leader's face grew as he watched her. He was happy to know that he affected her as much as she did him. Taking a drink of his coffee, he said, "Nyet. You will be safely locked away up here."

Piper nodded as she went back to eating her breakfast. She knew she should take comfort from Nikolai's words, but truth be told, she was scared. The blue-eyed blonde was not only scared for herself but for the man who sat across from her. When he'd leaned in to kiss her, Piper had wanted to crawl inside him and never leave. He made her feel so safe. She knew he would keep her secure and protected but what about himself? She really knew nothing about a bratva or what that entailed but had enough common sense to know that it was extremely dangerous. Nikolai was not only in a bratva, but he was its leader. She had no doubt that they would kill Paul and Grecoff quietly, but he was not indestructible. The last thing she wanted to see was this man get hurt. As much as she hated to admit it, Piper was beginning to care for him even if the feelings were not reciprocated. She had no idea how it was happening, but it was.

"Do you have any further questions regarding Paul and Grecoff?" When she shook her head, indicating that she didn't, he said, "Well, if you should, please don't hesitate to ask. I, of course, will keep you updated as we gather new information. Now let's move on to a different topic, shall we? Let's talk about last night. Why didn't you stay with me? Did you not enjoy the sex?"

Her platinum head shot up as he leaned back casually in his chair. She didn't want to be vulnerable and tell him the truth but there was no way she was going to lie. Dropping her fork and wiping her mouth, she sighed. "The sex was amazing! I mean, I don't even know if there is a word to describe how awesome it was. I left..." With another loud sigh, Piper shifted uncomfortably in her seat. "I left last night because I felt... I don't know what I felt but it was totally foreign and it scared me. I don't just sleep with random guys, let alone be the aggressor like I was last night. I have no idea what came over me. Maybe it was the wine, I don't know. All I do know is that I wanted you. Bad."

"And now?" Nikolai half-growled his question. His body was on fire hearing her say how much she wanted him. Her feelings mirrored his own. "Do you still want me?"

"Yes. Even more than last night," Piper whispered, seconds before he stood up and threw the table to the side, clearing the space between them. She was then jerked up from her seat and crushed in the Russian's strong, muscular arms. As his mouth devoured hers, he lifted her up under her bottom and pushed her back against the wall. Her legs wrapped around his waist tightly as her hands hungrily roamed his neck and back. She mated her tongue with his moments before he ripped the sports bra she wore over her head. Her small fingers frantically did the same and began removing his blazer and shirt. A moan escaped her lips when his hands found her breasts and he ravaged her neck and shoulders. She could feel how much he wanted her by the massive erection rubbing her core through his pants.

"Tell me to fuck you, sweetheart. Tell me you want me inside you," he groaned in her ear as her hand slid between their bodies and she began massaging his throbbing cock through the material. As she started to undo the zipper, he grabbed her hand to stop her actions. "No topping, pet. Tell me what you want."

"I want you inside me," she breathlessly moaned, as she was placed on her feet in front of him. She gasped when he quickly discarded her pants and picked her back up, only to press her back against the wall and wrap her legs around him once again.

Nikolai hurriedly pulled his thick, hard cock from his pants and rubbed the gigantic head against her clit. He loved the way her slick juices were coating both his large member and balls. Pulling her earlobe with his teeth, he roughly whispered, "Say 'I want you inside me, master. My pussy belongs to you.' Say those words exactly and you can have all of me."

When she felt the tip of his dick at the entrance to her opening, she could feel her own juices running down her inner thighs. Gripping his ebony hair, she brought his mouth to hers, only to pull at his lower lip with her teeth before licking the sensitive skin. Looking deep into his eyes, she groaned, "I want you inside me, master. My pussy belongs to you." Piper's head then fell back in pure ecstasy as the bratva leader eased every inch of himself into her cunt. The purr that escaped her lips was captured by his mouth finding hers. She then wrapped her arms around his neck and attempted to hold on as he began lifting her up and down his cock. She felt her impending orgasm as he bounced her faster and devoured her neck and breasts.

"Would my little lynx like to come on master's dick?" Nikolai asked gruffly, her sweet, tight pussy bringing his own orgasm closer to the edge.

"Yes, please, master," Piper moaned breathlessly as she rode him aggressively. "Let me come."

He then pinned her against the wall as he began pounding inside her pussy at a maddening pace. With each thrust of his hips, he brought her higher and higher, toward the pinnacle of release. Her panting and cries of passion grew with a lusty volume until she screamed out in euphoria as the blinding orgasm tore through her small frame. His growls and grunts mixed with her loud whimpers as her convulsing vaginal walls constricted around his dick and her juices flowed down his groin. She needed the muscles of his shoulders and neck as she rode the crest of explosive sensations her lover had caused. The black-haired Russian sucked on her nipples as the climax began to subside and her breathing began to normalize. However, before her body had fully relaxed, Nikolai lifted her off his cock, only to position her bottom side up against the railing.

"My turn, princess," he growled before he spread her ass cheeks wide and slid back into her tight, wet warmth. A shiver ran through him as her back touched his chest and her hands gripped painfully at his hair. As she did this, his hand slid down her breasts and stomach to slip into her pussy and manipulate her clit. She wiggled against him as he kissed her shoulder and the side of her neck. "Do you like the way I feel inside you?"

"Mmm. I love the way you feel, master. Fuck me hard, please."

Nikolai responded to her words by pushing her roughly over the railing and holding her there with his hand on the middle of her back. His balls slapped against her drenched pussy as he pumped himself deeper and deeper into her core. As he took her roughly, the head of his cock hit her G-spot in repetition. She set up her own rhythm in time with his and pushed back against his thrusts, adding to their pleasure. Sweat poured down his chest and onto her tanned, flawless skin as he rode her at a fevered pitch. He heard her cry out in another orgasm only seconds before her pussy tightened around his cock and he threw back his own head in surrender. He ground the entire length of himself in her snug heat as his own pleasure pulsated deep into her womb. The bratva leader moaned and tried to control his own breathing as he allowed the intense sensations to ravage his body. He pulled her back flush against his chest, only to turn her head toward him and kiss her passionately on the lips. As he did this, his hands massaged her breasts before he hugged her tightly to him.

"Well, that was magnificent." He smiled, kissing the pulse that beat wildly in her neck before nuzzling it.

"Yes, it was," Piper almost sang in satisfaction, wiggling her bottom against him before she kissed his lips. Her eyes then looked straight ahead before she screamed, "Oh my gosh! We just had sex on the balcony! Anybody could have watched us! What if someone recorded us?"

"Then let them. I hope they enjoyed it half as much as we did." He chuckled, amused by her sudden embarrassment. He then turned at the sound of someone approaching from inside. Slipping out of his woman's warmth with a grunt, he quickly fixed his pants and slid Piper behind him to shield her.

His tension suddenly eased as Mikhas stood there with a couple white robes.

"Sorry to bother you, Pakhan, but Chernoff is downstairs." The almost seven-foot-tall guard said, tossing his leader the robes. A small smile touched his lips when he saw the blonde standing on her toes to try to peek over Nikolai's shoulder. "Do you want me to send him up or ask him to wait?"

"Have him wait. Give me a minute and I'll meet you upstairs in my office."

"Da, sir."

As Mikhas left, Nikolai took one of the robes and opened it. As he turned around, he helped Piper slide into the fluffy, white material before hugging her close again. Kissing her softly on the lips, he smiled. "I'm sorry to leave you like this but I do have a meeting this morning."

"It's okay. I've already figured out that you are a busy man."

"I greatly enjoyed breakfast, though."

"So did I." She giggled, hugging his large, muscular body again.

"What do you have planned today?"

"I was thinking about calling my professor and talking to him. With everything going on right now and missing clinicals, I thought it might be a good idea to just drop classes this semester. I don't know, though. I thought it would just be a good idea to get his opinion on it. What about you?"

"I will be stuck in meetings all day, but I would like to take you out this evening," he said, watching her lovely face intently. "I would also like you to stay the night with me."

"I thought you said that is complicating things," she replied softly, casting her eyes down.

Nikolai lifted her chin so he could stare into her eyes. His voice was husky and deep as he said, "It is, but we did it anyway. We might as well enjoy the complication."

"Okay. I would like that," Piper replied, nodding her head before her mouth was captured in a hot, searing kiss. When he broke the kiss, she asked breathlessly. "Where are we going?"

"You let me take care of everything. The only thing you will need to do is head down to the boutique and purchase a dress. There will be a personal stylist waiting for you there as well. If you want it, sweetheart, it's yours."

"Thank you, Nikolai." She smiled, kissing him on the lips once more. She then cupped his face and forced him to look at her. "For everything, not just tonight. I don't know how I could ever repay you."

"You already have," the dark-haired giant said sincerely, touched by her gratitude and compassion. "There is one more thing that I want you to think about today."

"What's that?"

"I want you to be my submissive tonight, Piper," he said huskily, lust darkening his grey eyes. "I want to dominate you completely while you submit to my will. You will have to trust me in order to do this, baby." He could see the panic in her ocean-blue eyes, so before she could speak, he kissed her mouth lightly. "Just promise me that you'll think about it. You remember your safe word from last night, right? As I told you, that stops everything immediately. I can guarantee that you will enjoy every minute of it."

She stood there a moment and searched his eyes. She could tell that this was something he really wanted, and deep down, Piper wanted it too. She loved the way he dominated her during sex. Although being dominated was scary to her, she did find that she was beginning to trust Nikolai. She had never trusted anyone in her life, so the feeling was foreign and made her feel insecure. However, her desire for the man in front of her was greater than her fear. Biting her lip nervously, she said softly, "Okay, I promise I will think about it. Are you sure I would like it?"

"Positive." Nikolai smiled, displaying a row of straight, white teeth. He was overcome with joy with her even considering it. With a low growl, he kissed her passionately on the mouth once more and hugged her tightly before he released her and headed toward the door of the balcony. "I'll see you tonight, brat." And with that, he was gone.

Chapter 8

Piper stood back and admired her appearance in the boutique mirror as she turned from side to side. She couldn't believe how beautiful and regal she looked. The stylist Nikolai had sent her had really outdone herself. Her curly hair was pulled up in an elegant, curly, French twist updo and her makeup had been done in a soft, sultry look that defined her blue eyes even more. On her body, she wore a white halter-style dress that snugly fit her chest and flared out on the bottom. Her freshly painted toes were covered with a pair of navy-blue Manolo Blahniks that fit her perfectly. Wouldn't Andy just die if she saw her right now? She liked to dress up occasionally but even this was a bit much for her. As she stared at herself, Piper wondered if her lover would like what he saw.

"You really do look breathtaking, Ms. Williamson. You have an exquisite figure." The petite stylist smiled behind her in the mirror.

"Thank you for everything, Rosaline," she replied shyly, uncomfortable with the verbal praise. "You really did a wonderful job. I don't think I've ever looked this good before."

"Oh, I don't know about that. Something tells me you probably have." The older woman winked before she turned to grab a small box out of her bag. "Before I forget, there is one more thing that Mr. Volkov insisted that you wear tonight."

Taking the box from Rosaline, Piper looked at it a moment and suddenly became nervously excited. By looking at the size and shape of the box, she imagined what was inside was jewelry. Piper had always been so poor that she could never afford such a luxury. Even when she was able to make her own money, she never spent it on things like jewelry. Taking a deep breath, she opened the box and covered her mouth as she gasped loudly. Before her, sat a pair of stunning 2-carat diamond stud earrings with an equal sized oval sapphire teardrop hanging from the center stone. Below the earrings, lay a delicate oval sapphire and diamond tennis bracelet that was simply gorgeous. Quickly closing the box, she attempted to give it back to the stylist.

"I can't wear these," she blurted, shaking her head. "These must have cost Nikolai a fortune. I can't, I'm sorry."

"Mr. Volkov thought you might say that, so he told me to tell you that they are on loan for the evening." Rosaline smiled, pulling an earring from the box. With the shiny bobbles in her hand, she walked up to Piper and gently slid them on her ears. She then pulled out the bracelet and latched it on her wrist. Standing back to admire the blue-eyed goddess a moment, Rosaline beamed. "Well, that small addition gives you a touch of regality and nobility. The earrings do a nice job of bringing out your amazing blue eyes. I do believe Mr. Volkov knew what he was doing when he picked them out for you."

Piper said nothing in response to the stylist who began packing up her things. She fingered the expensive trinkets and again looked at herself in the mirror. She positively loved the jewelry and felt like a giddy schoolgirl with them, however, it also manifested alien emotions internally. The feelings Nikolai was provoking were not only strange but made her heart flutter and produced butterflies in her stomach. Since meeting the Russian in her condo two nights ago, there was a warmth that spread across her body every single time she thought about him. He was not only warm and kind, but she loved how affectionate he was with her, even when trying to reassure her. Deep down, she knew that going out with him tonight would complicate things even further but there was no way she was going to deny her heart what it wanted. Piper wanted this man, and even if it was temporary, she was going to enjoy every second.

"Well, Ms. Williamson, if you don't need anything further from me, it is time for me to leave. I hope you have a wonderful evening with Mr. Volkov." Rosaline smiled, standing with her bags. "I can show myself out and I will let the guards know that I am doing so. It was a pleasure."

"Thank you. It was nice to meet you as well," she replied softly. She then watched the older woman leave and Mikhas walk into the dressing room. She was unprepared for him just to stand there and stare at her with an odd look on his face. Unable to read his expression, she barked, "What the hell are you staring at? Don't like what you see?"

"No, quite the contrary, Piper," Mikhas replied, a huge smile spreading across his face. "You look wonderful! I'm sorry if I was staring but you are breathtaking. Niki will definitely approve."

She couldn't help the winsome smile that touched her lips as she broke eye contact with the guard and turned to grab the small clutch on the table. "Don't worry. All is forgiven. So, where are you taking me?"

"You'll see. Just follow me."

With anxious apprehension, Piper followed Mikhas out of

the room, down the elevator, and out to a waiting limousine. Climbing in the car, she expected to see Nikolai, but instead, found a dozen red Juliet roses. As the car took off and headed down the strip, she thought about her evening with the bratva leader and smelled the luxurious scent of the flowers. She felt good about herself, especially now that she had gotten a verbal compliment from his top guard. She knew she looked good and hoped that her lover liked what he saw. She had not physically seen him since their sexual encounter on the balcony, but she had not been able to shake his touch. Piper's body was still humming from the orgasms she had this morning, but also from the anticipation she was feeling for later this evening. She had already decided to try to trust Nikolai and allow him to dominate her tonight. Since she was novice to the position of submissive, she did have some questions she needed answered. Hopefully, the two of them could talk about that over dinner.

Feeling the car come to a stop and the door open, the American woman took the guard's hand and got out of the car. As they made their way toward the Las Vegas Eiffel Tower, Piper was quickly surrounded by four other men. She heard Mikhas say something to them in Russian before one of them pulled out his phone and quickly called someone. Instead of taking the entrance that everyone else was utilizing, she was led to a private elevator that she and the group boarded. She nervously began rubbing her arm as they made their way to the top. The men surrounding her were so serious and quiet that it made her even more anxious than when she was in the limo. Hopefully once she saw Nikolai, all of that would go away.

As the elevator doors opened, only Mikhas and Piper stepped off. They were greeted by a short, balding, middle-aged man who looked at her and said something in French that she didn't understand. When the man stopped talking, the guard said over his shoulder, "He was complimenting you on how you look. Thinks that you are a flower plucked from the very heavens. I think he is laying it on a little thick, don't you?"

A genuine smile touched her sultry red lips at the humor she heard in the guard's voice. She was grateful that he was breaking the tension. "Uh, yeah. I think someone is wanting a big tip."

Mikhas chuckled softly at her words before he said, "Okay, look. At this doorway up here, I'm going to leave and allow this gentleman to take you to Nik." He then turned his head to wink at her. "Welcome to the Top of the World, sweetheart. Enjoy your evening."

Piper watched the mountainous man walk away as she followed the shorter man into the restaurant. She felt the eyes of men and woman alike watching her curiously as she made her way across the expansive space. It didn't take long for her eyes to lock on Nikolai who stood beside their table dressed in a dark charcoal grey Brioni suit that also included a crisp, white shirt and a grey and blue tie. Her eyes scanned his delicious, muscular body that was barely contained under the Italian suit. He was well-manicured, aristocratic in appearance, and sinfully handsome. This man had a look that would stop any woman dead in her tracks, and tonight, he would belong to her. She could feel her vaginal walls constricting and weeping between her legs. Damn, tonight was going to be one for the history books!

When she reached Nikolai, she was immediately swallowed up in his arms as his mouth ravaged hers in a hungry kiss. She moaned into his mouth as his hands slid down her bare back and moved dangerously close to her bottom. However, before he mauled her right there in the room full of people, she felt him pull back and fight for control of his emotions. His grey eyes had darkened significantly with lust and by the way they were intently taking in every detail of her appearance, he more than approved.

Cupping her face in his hands, the bratva leader kissed her lips softly once more before they trailed a path to her ear. "There are not enough words for how magnificent you look tonight. Every man in this room is undressing you with his eyes, but I'm the only one who will get the actual pleasure."

"Maybe," she teased with a girlish giggle, loving the sexual tension vibrating between them. "That all depends on how the evening goes, Mr. Volkov. I must say, though, you look good enough to eat in that suit. Think I can have a taste later?"

"You can have a taste now if you like," he hungrily whispered in her ear as one long digit traced her nipple through the dress she wore. When a strong shiver ran through her body, he chuckled before he released her and stepped back. Pulling out a chair for her, a sexy grin played on his lips as she took a seat. "I'm glad to see that I affect you just as much as you do me. You are lucky, Ms. Williamson, that there is a room full of people watching us, or I would have you bent over this table right now. I am pleased with how exceptional you look this evening. I know I like, do you?"

Piper watched him take a seat across from her before reaching across the table to grab one of her hands. "I do, Nikolai. Everything about this outfit is amazing. I can't thank you enough. The flowers, the limo, everything… I will never forget this evening as long as I live."

Bringing her hand to his lips, he looked into her eyes and sincerely replied, "Neither will I, love." As he leaned in to kiss her lips, the waiter appeared to take their order. After asking for a bottle of their best champagne, Nik queried, "You haven't mentioned whether or not you like the jewelry yet. Is the jury still out on that?"

"No!" she exclaimed loudly. "I absolutely love them. I'm just overwhelmed with all of it. I know I'm now a millionaire but it's going to take some getting used to. I've never worn anything so expensive before. I'm just glad they're on loan."

Touched by the genuine display of joy and gratitude, Nikolai took out his phone and dialed the familiar number. Quickly saying something in Russian, he then hung up and winked at his lover. "They are on loan no longer. They now belong to you."

"Nikolai, no! I can't accept—"

"Da, you can, and you will," he defended, taking her hand once again as the waiter filled their glasses. "I won't take no for an answer. Now, tell me. How was your day, love?"

"Wonderful, thanks to you." She beamed, totally enamored with the man sitting across the table. "What about yours? How did your meetings go?"

"They went well. Were you able to speak to your professor today?"

"Yeah," she said, taking a drink of her wine. "After talking to him, I went ahead and dropped myself from the program."

"Why did you drop the program?" Nikolai asked, concerned, lifting his brow.

"I've just been doing a lot of thinking the past couple of days about the Paul situation and my life in general." She shrugged, rubbing her arms absently. "Andy and I had been talking about needing a change for a while now. She is basically done with her degree, and with my high MCAT scores and grades, I'm confident that I would be able to transfer to another medical program."

The grey-eyed colossus sat and contemplated Piper's words as the waiter came and took their order. He hated the touch of sadness he saw in her eyes and couldn't gauge how she was feeling. Plus, for a completely selfish reason, he could not imagine losing this woman from his life if he were unable to see her again. When the waiter walked away, he probed, "Are you that unhappy with things in your life, sweetheart? I can't help but see sadness in your eyes as you speak. Are you afraid of Paul and Grecoff? If so, let me reassure you that in a couple days, they will no longer be a threat. The last thing I want is for you to be afraid. Also, if you need anything from me, love, please do not hesitate to ask. If you plan on moving, I can help you relocate anywhere in the world."

With a sigh, she declared honestly, "I would be lying to you if I didn't admit that Paul and Grecoff scare me, but its more than that. This whole situation has given me an opportunity to assess myself on a personal level. My whole life has been a struggle, both emotionally and financially, and I'm tired of living that way. Thanks to you, I no longer will have to struggle financially, and I refuse to allow myself to continue the emotional battle when I don't have to. As for you offering help, I appreciate it, really, but I think this is something I need to do on my own. Anyway, enough about me. I would prefer we talk about you."

"You are very good at deflection, aren't you?" Nikolai remarked gently, reaching out to stroke her face affectionately. "You, my dear, have a bad habit of steering conversation away from yourself. I noticed it last night as we talked, and you are doing the same thing now. I want to get to know you, Piper. I understand that you're used to being judged, but I'm not going to do that to you. I would think I would have already proven that."

"It's not personal," she said uncomfortably as she pulled back slightly from his touch. "I just don't like talking about myself. I know it may sound cynical, but people say they want to know who you really are, but they don't actually care."

"Well, I'm not everyone else. Let's start with Andy. Tell me about your relationship with her."

"You're not going to let this go, are you?" she asked as he slowly shook his head. With a loud sigh, she blurted, "Fine. I'll tell you about Andy, but that it's for tonight. I thought we were supposed to be having fun. Talking about my past is anything but. Anyway, as you know, Andy is my stepsister. She was Maury's only biological child and came into my life when I was four. We were only together for about three years, but we were as close as peanut butter and jelly, you know? She was always trying to protect me from her father's violent episodes and even when she couldn't, she tried to patch me up and make me feel better."

"You mentioned Maury and his violent episodes, I take it he was abusive?"

"If he wasn't beating us, then we didn't know he cared," Piper replied softly, not able to keep eye contact with him. She hated talking about her past and was ashamed of it. "He was just like my mother, drunk or high all the time, but he preferred alcohol. Whiskey, to be exact. His rages always started after a night out with his friends. He would go out and then drink himself into a stupor for the next three or four days. Andy couldn't always keep me away from the initial part of his rages, but she became really good at hiding us away after they started. One time, he kicked me so hard that I passed out, and when I finally woke up, Andy had hidden me outside in a tent and her arm was broken. That was one of the last times he hit me before Mom died."

"Now I understand why you insisted that Andy have half of the money," Nikolai stated, taking a drink of his champagne. He knew the things this woman was saying were difficult, but he also understood how they had poisoned her emotionally over time. If Maury wasn't already dead, he would kill the son of a bitch himself. He would also make sure that Andy would be given anything she ever wanted.

"Without Andy, I wouldn't be here today." Piper half

smiled, thinking about her only family. "Plus, her life was worse than mine if you can believe that. When I turned eighteen, I had nowhere to go and had no clue how to navigate my way through life. As soon as I was released from the state's custody, Andy took me into her home and got me headed in the right direction. She has been by my side ever since."

At that moment, the waiter appeared and began placing their food in front of them. They both stared at each other without saying a word as they drank their champagne again. Before the waiter walked away, Nikolai had him bend down so he could whisper something in his ear. When the waiter walked away, he then leaned across the table and kissed her lips. He could see that she was waiting for him to judge her negatively, but there was nothing negative that he could say about the bombshell with eyes the color of the ocean. He admired her even more now, after her admission, than he did before. He knew her childhood had been bad, but she clearly suffered even more than he had suspected. Cupping her face, he stroked her jaw with his thumb and loved the way she placed a kiss on his palm. She also interlocked her hand with his. Knowing she needed the comfort, he stood up beside the table and reached out his hand to her. When the soft, melodic music began to play, she took his hand and was pulled into his strong arms. Nikolai then began to sway to the sound as he hugged her close to his body.

Piper sighed and fought back the tears that threatened to pour down her face as she hugged the Russian tight and danced in his arms. She knew the rest of the room was watching but she didn't care. Instead of judging her or patronizing her, Nikolai had simply pulled her into his arms and given her exactly what she needed, comfort. She blinked back the tears and inhaled his rich, masculine scent. The American medical student hated to admit it, but she was beginning to fall hard for this man. Right now, she wanted to jump up in his arms and wrap her legs around his waist as he buried himself inside of her. Her hands ran up his broad back to grip the black hair at the nape of his neck. She then lowered his head and captured his mouth with hers. Her tongue mated with his just as his hands trailed down her back and sides. She then broke the kiss to run kisses up his neck toward his ear.

On the edge of bending her over the table, he half-growled before he pushed her back roughly. With a wicked smile on his face, he huskily said in a low voice, "You'd better be glad that we are in a public restaurant because I would have already been balls deep inside you. I can guarantee that you will pay for that later tonight."

"Promise?" She smiled, hungrily licking her lips before she rubbed his face with hers. "How about you make me pay for it now?"

Kissing her lips once more, he tapped her nose with his finger before releasing her. He then walked around her and pulled her chair out again. He chuckled as he watched her pout and sit back down in the chair. When he took a seat, Nikolai could see the questions on her face. "As much as I want to fuck you right now, I'm not going to."

"Why?" she asked, suddenly feeling insecure.

"Because you want me to." He grinned, taking her hand to kiss her fingertips. "In my world, we call that topping from the bottom and that is not permitted. That type of behavior from a submissive is usually punished."

"But I haven't agreed to be your submissive yet," Piper said seriously, pulling her fingers back from his lips to pick up her fork. She then crossed her legs under the table and began to demurely eat her food.

"Have you at least thought about it today? You promised me that you would."

"I have but before I give you an answer, I have some questions."

Cocking a dark brow, he picked up his own fork and began to eat. "By all means, ask them."

"Okay, let's start with the safe word. You said if I say it at any time then everything stops, right?"

"Absolutely."

"What types of things are you into? I know some dominants like to do the humiliation and the bodily functions thing. Is that something you're into?"

"Nyet. I find that disgusting. I don't use sex to humiliate women," Nikolai responded sincerely, watching her face intently. "I use my position to please and punish my submissive. The punishment is typically something that you would find erotic. I like spanking, role play, flogs, bondage, toys. All done with your consent, of course."

Piper closed her eyes a moment as she took a deep breath. Her core pulsed in her underwear at the dirty thoughts and sensations his words were creating within her. Once she felt that her emotions were under better control, she opened her eyes and her pussy once again flooded at the hungry look she saw in the depths of his grey eyes. "If I let you do this, will you go slow?"

"Da. I'll go as slow as you need but I will push you if I feel like you can handle it. Being a submissive is something I think you will find quite enjoyable."

"Are there any rules I should know about?"

"Da. You must be open minded. When I speak, you obey and at no time will you dictate orders to me. You will ask me to orgasm unless I have already instructed otherwise. I will choose the area of your body that I will ejaculate on. You will communicate how you are feeling and lastly, make your master proud. If you make your master proud, you will be rewarded both in the bedroom and out."

"Will this submissive thing go beyond tonight?"

"That depends on you. I would like for it to. Who knows? Maybe I'll take you back to Russia with me."

Although Piper said nothing in response to Nikolai as she took a drink of her champagne, her heart was swelling with joy and excitement at his words. *Whoa, girl, calm down,* she chastised herself internally. She hadn't even been dominated by this man yet and here she was contemplating moving across the world. Did he want just a sexual relationship, or did he want something more? She had never been able to really explore her sexual appetites in the past with men and looked forward to doing so with Nikolai. Even if it was a temporary relationship, she would always have the memories. She was going to enjoy this man for however long she could and that would begin tonight.

Looking deep into his grey eyes, she took his hand in hers again and placed a kiss on its palm before sliding his thumb into her mouth to suck on. She stifled a giggle when she watched him clench his jaw and let out a low growl. Releasing his thumb out of her mouth, she said in a soft and sultry voice, "Okay, Master Nikolai. I will be your submissive tonight."

Nikolai moved uncomfortably in his seat as his cock slammed against the back of his pants. Damn, this woman drove him crazy and now she belonged solely to him! He intended on punishing her for that last little stunt and there was no time like the present. Clearing his throat, he said in a husky voice, "Then let's start now, shall we? I had already mentioned to you there is to be absolutely no topping from the bottom but that is exactly what you just tried to do. For that, you are to go to the restroom, remove your panties, and bring them back to the table. You will then hold them up for me to see. Understand?"

"What?" Piper gasped in shock as she let out an odd chuckle. "You're not serious, are you?" When he simply cocked his brow, she said, "I wasn't topping, or whatever you called it. I thought we would start once we got back to the hotel."

"We start whenever I say we start, my little lynx. Now go do as I say."

"Nikolai…"

Before she knew it, he was behind her and pulling out her chair. When she stood up, he wrapped his arms around her waist before he placed a chaste kiss on her neck. In her ear, he whispered, "You now belong to me, Piper. Remember, you do as I say without question. I don't want to punish you in front of all these people, but I will. Now be a good pet and go remove your panties."

Her body erupted into flames and her pussy drenched the G-string she wore as he sucked on her earlobe before pulling back to look at her sternly. She could tell by the glint in his eyes that he was serious and that this was no game. She knew people were watching them intently at this moment, but more so, she knew that Nikolai meant every word he had just said. Not wanting to disappoint him or be publicly punished, the blonde woman placed a kiss on his lips before she moved herself from his grasp and quickly made her way to the restroom. When she returned, she found the bratva leader sitting at the table casually eating his dinner. Taking her seat across from him, she placed the crumpled white cotton thong in her lap. Her heart was beating wildly in her chest when she looked at the Russian as he took a long drink of his champagne.

Wiping his mouth with the expensive linen, he asked simply, "Well?"

"I took them off like you said. They are in my lap."

"Hold them up for me to see."

Glancing around the room, Piper quickly held up the panties with both of her hands. Her vaginal walls twitched with raw, sexual need when he took the cotton from her hand and brought it up to his nose to smell. She then watched him stuff it in his jacket pocket as a hungry smile touched his lips. When he reached across the table and gripped her neck, the breath caught in her throat before he placed a sloppy, wet kiss on her lips.

Releasing her, he loved the perplexed look on her flawless face. He had smelled her arousal on the soft material and knew his American was sexually fueled. Even now, he could see her hard nipples poking through her dress and loved the way she was shifting in her seat because he had no doubt her beautiful cunt was throbbing. His own body was burning up, but he would make them both wait for any type of pleasure until they reached their suite. Then he would fully claim this delicious, tempting creature as his own. Knowing that she was antici-pating something further from him, he picked up his fork and instructed, "Eat, love."

"Eat? I don't know if I can," she answered honestly, her entire body aching with need.

"Yes, you can. Besides, you are going to need your strength for all that I have in store tonight for you, little one. Now do as I say."

"Y-yes." Piper nodded, picking up her fork as well.

"Yes, what?"

"Yes, master."

"Good girl." He winked, watching the blush cross her face. Little did she know it, but tonight was going to change Ms. Williamson's fate forever.

Chapter 9

Nikolai helped Piper into the limousine before climbing in himself. As soon as the door closed, he roughly pulled her onto his lap and passionately kissed her lips. She straddled his muscular thighs as his hands roamed her body and slipped under her dress to massage her breasts. She undulated her wet core against the massive, erect cock that lay beneath his expensive suit. When he plucked at her nipples with his thumb and forefinger, she gasped and broke the kiss just as he breathlessly said, "Sit back on the seat with your dress up and your legs spread wide. I want to taste my pussy."

Piper quickly did as her lover commanded. Her pussy dripped with need and glistened with moisture as Nikolai's eyes devoured it. She waited with bated breath as he slowly approached her from the other side of the car. He had not touched her since taking her panties from her and had kept the conversation relatively neutral. Piper wouldn't tell the bratva leader this, but the remainder of the dinner had been absolute torture. She had attempted to touch and kiss him several times, but Nikolai would not allow it. She had not only wanted to devour him, but she also wanted the giant in her and on her. Her body had almost had an orgasm as she undulated her hips against his. She was ready to explode and would take matters into her own hands if he didn't help her soon.

The voluptuous woman cried out in ecstasy when the Russian's two fingers slid into her pussy and he began moving them in and out slowly. As he fucked her with his fingers, his thumb playfully rubbed against her clitoris. Baring one breast with his free hand, Nikolai's hot tongue lapped at her rose-colored nipple. She gripped the front of his jacket and tried to undulate her hips against the fingers manipulating her. Piper then gasped when his free hand came down painfully on the cleanly shaven mound and his tongue pulled away from her breast.

"Give me your hands, pet," he commanded. When she did, Nikolai reached into his pocket and pulled out the thong she had given him earlier before he bound her hands together. When he saw the pout on her red lips, he smiled. "You can touch me later. Right now, I want your hands above your head."

Piper let out a loud moan and her bound hands gripped the seat behind her head when her silver-eyed lover pulled her hips closer to the edge and his mouth found her core. As his tongue caressed the hard, wet nub, his eyes watched her struggle against the restraint and his mouth. She moved her pussy in time with his tongue and lips as they sucked and played with the apex of her vagina. Without thought and on pure, emotional overload, she purred, "Please let me come, baby. Please."

"Please, what?" he asked, pulling his mouth from her warmth to kiss her inner thighs. He then slid two of his fingers back into her opening as her eyes locked with his. "You know what I want to hear. Your master needs to hear you beg."

"Please, master," the American begged, lifting her hips up

and down so his fingers could go deeper. "Please let your submissive come in your mouth."

"Good girl. You are learning fast." Nikolai smiled, running his tongue up her vaginal lips. "Now come, my little lynx. Come in my mouth."

She heaved a euphoric sigh of relief as her lover began to fuck her faster with his fingers and mouth. Piper squirmed against his face as he devoured her essence. She felt the impending orgasm growing in her loins as he pleasured her, and she fought against the restraints. She wanted to bury her bound hands in his hair but innately knew that he would stop his actions if she did, and she wanted to find a release. With one final thrust of his fingers and tongue, an agonized howl escaped her lips as the climax tore through her voluptuous body. Her juices flowed into Nikolai's mouth as he drank the sweet fluid, and she fought the darkness that threatened to overtake her. As she floated above her body, she felt him trail a path of kisses up her stomach, breasts, and neck. A blissful murmur escaped her lips when his mouth finally found hers and kissed her passionately.

"Mmm. You taste like warm honey." The bratva leader grinned, running his tongue along her bottom lip as he removed the panties from her wrists. "Did my mouth feel good?"

"It felt amazing, master," Piper cooed, rubbing herself against him like a well-fed cat. She then pushed him back on the couch and got down on her knees between his open thighs. Placing a kiss on his lips, she breathlessly whispered, "May I please you now, sir? Please allow me to taste you."

The ebony-haired giant stared into eyes the color of a calm ocean as he released the clip from her hair and massaged the scalp. This woman made it difficult to breathe. For someone who was unsure about becoming a submissive, she was falling perfectly into the role. Relaxing back against the back of the seat, he gripped her neck loosely and brought her up so he could kiss her lips. "Take me in your mouth and suck me off. I want you to drink every drop."

A warm, sexual smile touched her lips before her eyes dropped to the bulge resting between his legs. As she began to unbuckle his pants with her petite hands, she rubbed her tanned, flawless face against the inside of his muscular thighs. Her hand trembled as she pulled out the large, rock-hard cock and began gently stroking it. Piper then lovingly rubbed it against her lips and face as she looked deep into Nikolai's dark eyes. She then dipped her blonde head to lick his balls and suck the sensitive skin into her mouth. The submissive then hid a giggle as she heard her lover groan when she ran her tongue along the slit of his cock. Tasting the precum, she edged the tip of the head before she took it into her mouth. She felt his hips instinctually flex up as she then eased the entire length into the back of her throat.

Nikolai gripped her platinum hair in his hands as she set up a rhythm with her mouth. He moaned and bucked uncontrollably as his woman deepthroated his dick and massaged his balls. She sucked him with a mounting fever and gusto as the explosive feeling began to grow in his groin. He pumped himself harder and faster into her mouth as she moaned and purred in pleasure and coaxed him to be more aggressive. She then popped him out of her mouth to nibble a path down the vein on the underside of the velvety skin. Just as she put the tip of his cock back into her mouth, he cursed and grunted loudly as the cum exploded from the slit. His head fell back, and his grip immediately loosened on her hair as she sucked every drop from the silky skin. Taking the softening member from her mouth, Piper kissed the tip of it before she was pulled up into his arms and hugged tightly.

"Did I please you, master?" She giggled as a lazy, soft smile played on his lips before he kissed her gently.

Letting out a relaxed exhale, he traced the lines of her beautiful face with the tip of his index finger. "Da. Immensely. Your mouth felt wonderful."

"So did yours." She smiled before kissing his mouth again. "What are our plans for the rest of the evening?"

"As soon as we get back to the hotel, you are going to take off your clothes and I am going to dominate you for the rest of the evening."

"I can't wait," she returned as the limo they were in came to a stop.

Just then, the door to the limo was opened and Nikolai got out of the car before taking her hand and pulling her out as well. The two walked arm in arm, talking and laughing lightly as they made their way up through the crowded casino and up the elevator to their room. Once the sliding door opened, the Russian whispered in Piper's ear before he pulled her into the suite and the couple quickly made their way to his bedroom. When they entered the room and the door closed, he pushed her body up against the wood and began to consume her mouth with his.

Feeling her body slump against his, he pushed back and lifted her chin so he could look deep into her eyes. Searching them a moment, he asked sincerely, "Are you sure you want to do this? There is no turning back once you become my submissive, Piper. All of you will belong to me. Are you ready for that?"

"Yes," she whispered breathlessly against his mouth. "I want you, Nikolai, more than anything I have ever wanted in my life."

"Then you shall have me." He smiled, soothing a fallen strand of hair from her face. "But first, I want to watch you take off your clothes." He then released her and removed his suit jacket before laying it across the back of a comfy leather chair. As he took a seat, he began unbuttoning his linen shirt before he pulled it off too and discarded it on the floor. Motioning to Piper, he watched her slowly begin to raise her dress up before she jerked it over her head. His mouth went dry as his eyes scanned perfect tanned breasts, wide hips, and a beautiful blonde landing strip on the apex of her womanhood. She was the most stunning woman he had ever taken to his bed. There was something about her body that made every nerve ending in his body spark with electricity and lust and now she belonged to him.

"Do you like what you see, master?" Piper asked shyly, her body on fire as he approached her, only to walk around her without touching her. "I hope my body pleases you."

"Oh, your body pleases me greatly, pet." Nikolai chuckled, loving the way her hair fell over her shoulders. He then stood behind her and moved the fallen strands to the side before sucking on her neck, directly below her right ear. Then in her ear, he whispered, "In fact, your body is perfect."

A blush spread over her skin as she watched her lover stand before her and strip off the rest of his clothes. She rubbed her legs together as a painful ache set up in her pussy. This man's body was muscular, magnificent, and sexy as hell. When her eyes locked on the large organ that brought her so much pleasure, her fingers instinctually shot to her throbbing clit. She barely caressed the tiny, hard nub when Nikolai's hands gripped her wrists, and she was dragged against his hard body.

"Did I give you permission to touch yourself?" he asked angrily, his mouth only centimeters from hers.

"No, sir."

"My submissive is intentionally being disobedient to her master." The Russian seductively smiled, tracing one pert nipple as his other held hers in place. "I think someone wants to be punished. Let's make that happen, shall we?"

Piper couldn't help the sexual apprehension that was

building in the pit of her stomach as her lover walked her over to the modern king-sized bed. She watched him grab his shirt off the floor before he bound her hands together behind her back, then he bent her over the side of the bed. A shiver shot through her body as his hand trailed down her back to her bottom. When his fingers slid down the crack of her butt and slipped into her vaginal opening, a loud moan escaped her lips. His long, slender fingers slid in and out of her wetness a moment before his other hand came down painfully on her backside. She cried out in a mixture of pleasure and pain before he released her and walked away from the bed. Craning her head sideways, she watched Nikolai go over to a drawer and pull out a red and black flog whip. Seeing him approaching her with the sex toy, made her immediately want to scream out her safe word, but she told herself to trust him and breathe.

"Such soft, flawless skin," the bratva leader said gently as he trailed the leather tresses down her back and butt. A soft chuckle escaped his lips when he saw her flinch slightly and fight against the bind. Just because she was anticipating it, he lightly flogged her backside twice. Even though she cried out in discomfort, the moisture from her pretty cunt slid down her inner thighs. Bending down, he placed a kiss on the area that he had just touched. He then ran the shaft of the toy between her vaginal lips before he circled her clit with the end of it. Placing a kiss on the middle of her spine, he asked, "Do you want me to quit, pet?"

An agonized cry of pleasure fell from her lips before she whispered, barely audible, "N-no. Please punish me, master."

Nikolai's response was to flog her backside several more times, each time a little harder than the last. This time as he struck her, his fingers manipulated the sensitive, enlarged nub that lay deep in her pussy. He could tell by her breathing and the flushed tone of her skin that Piper was extremely close to having an orgasm. His own cock throbbed with desire and anticipation as his new submissive inched closer and closer to her release. Fuck, she was magnificent to watch! He had anticipated that his little blonde American would have already said her safe word, but clearly something had transpired between the two of them tonight that made her feel as though she could trust him.

"Master," she softly moaned, her body close to the edge of an overwhelming release. The sexual rapture she felt mixed with the pain of the flogging was unlike anything she had ever experienced before. "I don't think... I can take... much more."

"Is my little lynx hurting?" he asked, spanking her again with the flogger. When a tormented cry fell from her lips, he chuckled. "I'll take that as a yes." Tossing the flogger aside, he trailed kisses up her back and shoulders as his fingers quickened their manipulation. In her ear, he urged, "Come for me, pet. Come hard."

As if on command, Piper screamed out as the glorious orgasm ripped through her and her essence gushed down her legs. She panted and jerked as her vision tunneled and the intensity of her release had tears running down her beautiful face. She swore for a moment that she could see stars floating around the room before she buried her face into the covers. Her body rode the wave of pure bliss as she struggled against the shirt he used as a restraint. As her vaginal walls convulsed, the blue-eyed angel felt Nikolai position himself behind her before he spread her legs wide and eased his cock deep into her dripping wet canal. His massive, erect member filled her completely as the two of them sighed in luxury. He then pulled all but the head of his cock out of her before he plunged back into her warmth. The muscular dominant did this several times to extend her orgasm before he set up a hard, fast, intense rhythm. As his balls slapped her ass, she cried out a second time as another orgasm hit her hard. He roughly jerked her body back and forth on his dick and gripped her hips almost painfully until, with one final push, she felt his seed pumping deep into her womb as a loud, primal growl escaped his lips. Her lover collapsed on top of her, murmuring words in Russian that she did not understand. She then felt his lips brushing the skin of her shoulders and neck as he allowed his own orgasm to fill her and his breathing to become normal.

After what seemed like an eternity of rapture, Nikolai rose and quickly undid the binding on her wrists. He gave her a minute to stretch her arms before he scooped her up in his arms and laid her in the center of the bed. His body quickly covered hers as the two passionately kissed and they entwined their arms around each other. He raised himself up on his elbow so he could stare into her lovely face. The bratva leader could not even begin to understand what he was feeling in that moment, but he knew that he never wanted it to end. Bending his head down, he captured her lips once more in a kiss. When he pulled back this time, he could tell that his new submissive was somewhere in her head. He would have to break her of that horrible habit.

A shiver ran through her body, causing goose pimples to form across her skin as her lover placed a kiss on each of her breasts and got up out of the bed. Sitting up quickly, she shyly asked, "Where are you going?"

"I'm getting us something to drink." Nikolai smiled as he glanced back at her. "Would you like a glass of wine?"

"Um, I think I would rather have some ice water," she replied, trying to cover her breasts with her arms.

"If you're cold, love, pull back the covers and crawl under. I'll be right with you."

Piper did as he instructed and quickly slid under the warmth of the covers. Truth be told, she wasn't really cold, but she was feeling extremely insecure suddenly. Taking the glass of water from him, she took a drink as he crawled into the bed. She then watched him down half the glass of vodka before he set it on the bedside table. She allowed him to take her glass of water as well for just a second before he lay back on a mound of pillows and pulled her across his lap. Her pussy immediately began to moisten when she felt his muscular eight pack beneath her. Because she needed the contact, she bent her head and hungrily kissed his lips. When she pulled back, she began tracing the intricate, elaborate tattoos on his chest. She had a million questions she wanted to ask him but had no idea how to break the comfortable silence.

"I can tell by the look on your face that although you are physically in this bed with me, mentally, you are somewhere else." He smiled, playing with a strand of her blonde curls. "What's on your mind, sweetheart? There are not supposed to be any secrets between a dominant and his submissive."

Her face flushed with color as her eyes met his. "I'm not sure how to ask this so I just will. Did you like it? I mean, did I make a good submissive?"

"You couldn't tell? I thought I made it pretty obvious how much I enjoyed it."

"I'm not talking about having an orgasm, I mean that is the pinnacle of sex anyway. With it being my first time, did I do everything right? How do I compare to your other submissives?"

Nikolai gripped her neck loosely as he brought her head down and passionately captured her mouth. His tongue mated with hers before he pulled back and whispered next to her mouth, "You were exquisite, Piper, and just so you know, there is no comparing you to my other submissives because you are one of a kind. I've never felt anything so sexually intense before. There is no way I can put it into words."

"Really?" she asked with a breathtaking smile on her face. "You're not just saying that?"

"Nyet. I gained your complete trust, sweetheart. You have no idea how special that is to me. I promise you I will never break that," he said softly, searching her eyes as he saw tears brimming there. He could see how much his words meant to her and that made his heart swell with love and pride. Wiping at her eyes with his thumb, he queried, "Did you enjoy it?"

"That was amazing!" Piper giggled, cupping his face before she kissed his mouth. "I can't believe I judged the life-style so harshly. Clearly, I didn't know what I was talking about. Either that, or you are just an exceptional Dom."

"I'm an exceptional Dom." Nikolai laughed, glad to see the tension draining from her body and a smile on her pretty face.

"A little too cocky, aren't you?"

"I believe I've earned the right to be. I've never had a complaint in the sexual department before."

"No, I'll bet you haven't. I imagine most women take one look at that handsome face of yours and melt into a puddle." Piper grinned, circling his nipples with her fingernail as his hands trailed down her sides to her bottom. "Can I ask you a question while we are on the subject of other women?"

"Of course. What's on your mind?"

"Can we be exclusive while you are here in the States? I mean, I don't plan on having sex with anyone else and was just thinking that you would grant me the same courtesy. As soon as you take care of Paul and Grecoff, you can go back to doing whatever you like."

Nikolai responded to her by spreading her wet pussy wide and sliding her down his erect cock. When he was firmly buried deep inside her warmth, he cupped her face and ardently devoured her mouth. When he broke the kiss, he nuzzled her neck as he whispered, "You're the only one I want, Piper. I'm yours, and yours alone, as long as you want me." He saw the tears leap to her eyes as he started to move her tight canal up and down his shaft. Capturing her mouth again, he whispered, "Do you need me, sweetheart?"

"Yes, master. I need you."

"Then show me how much."

Piper then pushed Nikolai back on the pillows. Her hands kneaded his muscular, tattooed chest before she began undulating her hips against his. She threw her head back as she bounced on his cock, enjoying the exquisite feeling of her lover deep inside her. As she began to quicken her pace, the Russian gripped her large, tanned breasts in his hands just as his hot mouth found her neck and shoulders. Throwing her arms around his neck, she massaged his shoulders as droplets of sweat formed on her back. As she rode him with deep, long thrusts, Piper tightened her vaginal muscles to bring each of them more pleasure. Needing to find her release, she roughly pushed him back against the pillows and connected her eyes with his. She then rocked her hips back and forth and in a circular motion that inched her closer and closer to an orgasm.

"Keep your eyes on me when you come, love. Understand?"

"Y-yes, sir," she purred, keeping her eyes locked with his. She then felt his hands gripping her hips as he aided her rocking motions and helped her toward the pinnacle. Then in one swift motion as she came down again on his cock, she screamed out as the intense wave of pleasure crested and her essence slid down her vaginal walls and pooled on the base of his dick. Piper's body jerked and shook as she rode the immense feelings of delight and bliss as he continued to manipulate her movements but slowly and methodically. Just as she felt herself coming back down from the clouds, she was rolled under Nikolai as he pumped himself inside her at a frantic pace. Within minutes, Piper was yelling out his name again as the second orgasm shook her body. She accepted all his body weight as he hooked one of her legs around his waist and pounded deeper and deeper into her pussy. Her fingers pulled at the damp strands of black hair at the nape of his neck as she moaned and whimpered in pleasure. Then in one final push, her lover growled loudly like a wild animal and ejaculated deep into her core. She placed soft kisses on his face and neck as he ground himself inside her womb and allowed every drop to flood her channel. She snuggled against his bare, tattooed chest as his arms engulfed her. As Piper drifted off to sleep, she smiled at the thought of also falling in love.

Chapter 10

Piper stretched out her curvaceous, naked form in the large king-sized bed as she rolled over on her back. Opening one eye, she could see the brilliant sunlight streaming in from behind the curtains that were automatically separating. Glancing at the clock on the bedside table, she sat up when she saw the time, 11:00 am. Where was Nikolai and why did he not wake her up this morning? The couple had spent the last two days together, both in bed and out. After going out to dinner and then submitting to her lover two nights ago, they had been almost inseparable. They had become so close in such a short time that she had found herself falling hard for the Russian. He had shared so much personal information with her about his family and his business that Piper had felt compelled to do the same. Not once, had he judged her or pitied her. He had simply been wonderful, compassionate, and understanding.

A smile touched her lips as she thought about the gorgeous bratva leader while she stretched out on the plush pillows. She couldn't even count the number of times they'd had sex over the past two days. Her dominant had made her do things she had only dreamed about doing. She hadn't used her safe word or even thought about it. He had made her feel so comfortable, even with the spankings and floggings. The orgasms were always uber intense and he gave as much as he took. She had never really enjoyed sex with her other partners, but with Nikolai, she craved the intimate contact. She was trying not to complicate their relationship, but the truth was it already was. Piper was having feelings for her grey-eyed lover that she had never experienced before. She found herself caring for him more than she even wanted to admit and the thought of never seeing him again broke her heart in two. They had not talked about their current relationship or where it could potentially go. The blue-eyed vixen had no idea where Nikolai stood emotionally and was afraid to ask.

Hearing a soft knock on the bedroom door, she covered herself modestly and yelled, "Come in." She was surprised to see Mikhas standing there with an envelope in his hand. She watched him place it on the large shelf by the door before he smiled at her and left the room. Piper quickly jumped out of the bed and wrapped the sheet around herself before grabbing the envelope and ripping it open. It was a note from her dominant that read: *Get cleaned up and meet me downstairs for lunch. We need to talk, and soon. Love, Nikolai.* With a girlish giggle, she threw off the sheet she was wrapped in and quickly made her way to the bathroom. When she kicked on the water, the steam billowed out of the multiple shower heads as she allowed the hot, clear liquid to soothe her sore, aching body. She was anxious to see Nikolai but worried about what he had to say. He had already told her last night that Paul and Grecoff were arriving today, as well as his brother Aleksandr. She knew the Volkov brothers had been in constant contact but didn't know the particulars of the plan. Maybe that was part of what he wanted to talk to her about. Was she ready for that?

With a loud sigh, Piper finished her shower and turned off the water. Tying the towel around her waist, she walked to the vanity where she wiped the steam from the mirror and looked at her reflection. For the first time in her life, she saw true happiness deep in her eyes. Along with the happiness, though, there was also a sadness creeping into their blue depths. Her life had changed so much since meeting Nikolai and although she didn't understand it, he made her feel lighter... loved. Although she had known him for only a few days, it was already hard to picture her life without him in it. With the arrival of Paul and Grecoff, today would be the last day her lover would have to be here in America. Would he still want her once her stepbrother and associate were dead? Did he want a relationship with her beyond today? If he did, could she even handle being with someone who lived his type of life? The thought of him always being in danger or someone hurting him terrified her to the core. If something happened to him, well, the thought was too painful to finish. She wasn't sure how it had happened, but Piper Williamson had fallen in love with Nikolai Volkov.

Shaking herself mentally, the young American woman finished getting ready and putting on her makeup before she took one last look at herself in the full-length mirror. She approved of the light blue, paisley knee length dress and the vintage style, platinum, diamond necklace that Nikolai had given her last night. Piper had been completely taken off guard when he had given her the necklace and overcome with emotion at how beautiful it was. At first, she had declined the gift, but he would not take no for an answer. Now, she never wanted to take it off. With one last smile at her appearance, she slipped on her light blue canvas shoes and went looking for Mikhas.

A few minutes later, Piper was being led into a small café at the base of the hotel by Mikhas and a handful of guards.

Her eyes immediately touched on her dominant who was engaged in what looked like a serious conversation with a handful of men. Her eyes wandered down his giant, muscular form that wore a pair of jeans and a light blue, long-sleeved linen shirt. Even though he was casually dressed, one would easily know that he was the leader in the small group. His shirt sleeves were rolled up to the elbows, exposing colorful tattoos. When he glanced her way and smiled, she instantly clenched her vaginal walls together as they began to pulse. God, this man made her heart skip a beat with just a single look! Even now, she wanted to run to him and beg him to make love to her.

"Mmm," Nikolai moaned as he dismissed the men he was talking to and quickly approached her. Once he reached her, he pulled her into his arms and passionately captured her lips. "You look delicious this morning, my little lynx. I take it you slept well."

"Too good, actually," Piper replied, fingering his clean-shaven jaw. "I think our sexual marathon wore me out."

"Well, make sure to get plenty of rest today because I have something extra special in mind for tonight." He winked, kissing her lips once more. He then grabbed her hand and pulled her behind him, saying, "Come on. Let's get some food in that belly. I'm hungry so I know you are."

She laughed loudly as she walked behind him. "What exactly are you trying to say about me, Mr. Volkov?"

"Only that you might be a bigger foodie than I am, my dear," he teased, using the American slang word she had taught him. "I have a treat for you this morning. I was craving some Russian home cooking so had some things prepared for us. I hope you like them."

She took the seat he pulled out for her and instantly smelled the delicious aroma of the food. Her mouth watered as she looked around the table. "It looks fabulous. Did you cook this?"

"Nyet." Nikolai chuckled. "I enjoy eating food, but I am horrible at cooking it. You can thank Krugan for this delicious meal."

"Who is Krugan?"

"He is one of my best men and a very dear friend. I'm sure you'll meet him soon."

"I look forward to it. Now what am I about to eat? It smells wonderful. I just hope it tastes as good as it looks."

"Oh, it will. Now let's see." He pointed to the items on the table. "This is kotleti. It's a type of fried chicken with onions and breadcrumbs. Then we have blini which is like a crepe, filled with all kinds of meats, eggs, caviar, and honey. Then lastly, we have some pickled vegetables. Dig in, my little lynx."

Piper quickly made her plate before making one for him as well. Her head fell back in pleasure, and a moan escaped her lips as she bit into the amazing food. Doing a little dance in her chair, she looked at her lover and sighed. "Mmm, this is so good!"

Nikolai laughed at her actions as he, too, bit into the tasty food. She clearly was enjoying the tastes of his homeland and that made him happy, especially since he planned on having her come back to Russia with him. "I'll have to tell Krugan that you approve of his cooking." His tone then took on a rather serious note as he reached across the table and took her hand in his. "We need to talk about today, sweetheart."

Hearing the urgency in his tone, made her heartbeat quicken and her pulse begin to race. This was the last thing she wanted to talk about but knew it was important that they do so. Maybe she could convince Nikolai somehow that he could stay with her instead of putting himself in harm's way. Squeezing his hand in hers, she asked, "What exactly do we need to talk about?"

"We received word that Paul and Grecoff are now here in Las Vegas. Zan and I have scheduled a meeting with them at an abandoned casino later today. My brother will be arriving in an hour and it is important that he and I finalize our plan before we meet with them."

"Why are you going to meet them face to face?" she asked, fear evident in her voice and eyes. "You know they want you both dead so why would you meet with them? Can't you just send men to kill them or something? Why do you need to endanger yourself?"

"Because that is bratva culture, sweetheart." He sighed, as she pulled her hand away from his. He hated the worry he saw on her lovely face. "I know you don't understand our way of doing things although I have tried to explain it to you. Yes, they want us dead and have gone to great lengths to destroy us, but unlike them, Zan and I fight with integrity and honor. We anticipate betrayal and have already factored that into our plans. If we don't fight Paul and Grecoff head on, then the underworld will view us as weak, and that cannot be allowed."

"I understand what you're saying, Nik, but who will know if you do things differently while you're here?" Piper exclaimed as she pushed her plate away and leaned back in her chair. "I don't see why you have to put yourself in danger, baby. You already know these are men who don't abide by any sort of rules or code."

"I'll know, dammit!" Nikolai declared angrily as he shot to his feet. "Volkov men don't back down in the face of danger, nor do we send our men out to do something that we wouldn't do ourselves. Look, I don't expect you to understand my actions, Piper, but I do expect you to support them."

"But I'm scared!" she blurted out as she, too, jumped to her feet. She could not stop the tears that began to fall down her face. "I don't want anything to happen to you. I know we haven't known each other long, but I..."

Walking up to her, the dark-haired Russian immediately pulled her struggling frame into his arms before he brushed the tears from her cheeks. He felt her body trembling against his chest as he allowed her to cry. After a few minutes of silence, he brushed the hair from her face as he looked deep into her eyes. "What were you going to say, Piper? Finish your sentence."

She exhaled shakily as her eyes searched his. She wanted to scream that she loved him but would not allow herself to do so. What if he rejected her? What if he didn't feel the same? No, she couldn't take that risk right now. It was just too soon. With a voice barely above a whisper, she said, "I care about you, Nikolai. I know we haven't known each other more than a few days but I won't deny that I have developed feelings for you. I know I probably sound crazy, and I don't expect you to reciprocate them but—"

"But I do," Nikolai interjected softly, stroking her jawline with his thumb. "You're right, sweetheart. There has been nothing ordinary about any of this, but I care about you, too. I had planned on having this conversation with you tonight, but I would like for you to fly back to Russia with me." When she opened her mouth in surprise to speak, he urged, "Before you answer me, I want you to think about it first. I know I am asking a lot of you but promise me you will at least think about it."

"Nik, this is crazy!" She began shaking her head in disbelief as she pushed against his chest. However, before she could pull away from him, his mouth captured hers in a hungry, passionate kiss. She returned the kiss with all the fire and emotion he was giving her. Her arms wrapped around his neck as his hands slid under her thighs and he picked her up before he sat her on the table. His fingers ran up her bare thighs and quickly spread her legs wide before wrapping them around his waist. As he spread her wide, Piper feverishly unbuckled his belt and pants and pulled his erect, thick cock free. She felt the precum oozing from its mushroom-shaped head as she pulled her underwear aside and rubbed it against her throbbing nub. A low, primal growl fell from his lips as he smacked her hand away from his dick before he positioned it at the entrance of her opening and pushed himself inside. The gorgeous blonde held Nikolai tightly and moaned in ecstasy as he roughly fucked her pussy. All her mixed emotions poured into him as she devoured his mouth with hers.

Fighting for control of his own emotions, he slowed his pace as he tried to also slow his ragged breathing. As he broke the kiss, he dragged his lips and tongue down her neck as he circled his hips against hers, prolonging their pleasure. At her ear, he groaned, "Does that feel good, my little lynx?" When he heard her whimpers, he chuckled. "If you want to feel your master deep in that pretty cunt, then you will think about Russia. Tell me what I want to hear, and we can come together."

"I... can't," she said breathlessly as he stopped moving inside her. When she tried to move her hips instead, his hand came down hard on the mound of her pussy as she cried out. "Please, master, please. I need you."

"Then let me hear the words, pet." He grimaced, pulling her earlobe with his teeth. It was so painful not to move inside her, but they both would suffer until he heard what he wanted from her lips.

"I p-promise," she begged just as his fingers began manipulating her clit, "I swear, master. Now fuck me, baby. Fuck me hard."

Nikolai didn't recognize his own groan as he plunged balls deep back into her warmth. He allowed himself to drown in his feelings for her as he roughly took her on the table. Although he wasn't ready to admit it, the bratva leader was falling in love with Piper Williamson. She had given herself to him completely in the last few days and, with that, had come her full trust. He would never forget the night she submitted to him fully. The emotions had almost been too intense to bear. Even now, his heart threatened to beat out of his chest as he made love to her. He felt her nails scratching down his muscular back seconds before his submissive screamed and the intense orgasm claimed her. As she came hard, she clenched her walls down on his cock and reached between them to massage his testicles. At that moment, Nikolai threw his own head back and shot his load inside her womb. The two held each other tightly and caressed their tongues together as her body milked his. He could feel the wetness there from her tears as she buried her face against his chest.

After a moment of silence, the Russian lifted her chin and kissed her lightly on the lips. Searching her eyes again, he gently queried, "Why are you crying, sweetheart? Tell me what is making you sad."

"I'm scared, baby," she replied, whisper soft. "I don't want to lose you. If something happens to you today—"

Nikolai silenced her words with a kiss before he said, "You won't, love. There is nothing that will keep me away from you, especially someone like Paul or Grecoff. Do you trust me?"

"Yes, I do. If I didn't, I wouldn't have agreed to be your submissive."

"Then trust me to come back to you."

"Okay," she said with a sigh as she rubbed her nose against his. "Promise me, though, that you'll be safe."

A gentle, heartwarming smile crossed his lips before he placed a kiss on her neck. "I promise." He then pulled his softening cock from her pussy as a shiver ran down his spine. Fixing his pants, he grabbed her hands and helped Piper off the table. He then pulled her back into his arms and kissed her lips again. "I'm sorry to do this, my little lynx, but I have to go. Mikhas will take you back up to my suite where a surprise is waiting for you. I won't be able to call you, but I will be home sometime tonight. You are not to leave the suite for any reason until I tell you otherwise. Understand?" When she nodded her head in response, he looked into her eyes and said sternly, "Give me your word. I want to hear that you won't leave the suite."

"Okay," Piper replied, rolling her eyes in agitation. "I give you my word. I won't leave the suite."

They hurriedly dressed then.

Just then, Mikhas walked into the room with two large men. Piper hugged her lover tightly to her chest once more before she reluctantly released him and headed toward the guards. Before exiting the room, she turned and looked at him once more before blowing him a kiss. Her blue eyes immediately teared up seconds before the clear liquid fell down her face. She stood in the elevator and hugged herself a moment as she allowed herself the luxury of crying. She was unprepared to feel the hand touch her back gently before being handed a handkerchief. Without looking at Mikhas, she whispered, "Thank you."

"Don't cry, little one," the mountain of a man responded gently. "I have known Niki for several years and he will return to you. There is no need to worry about his safety."

The woman said nothing in response to the guard as she wiped the tears from her eyes with the expensive pocket linen. She and the other men then stood in silence as the elevator slowly made its way to the top floor. Piper was so engrossed in her own thoughts when she entered the suite that she walked past the person sitting on the couch. Hearing the familiar voice say her name, she turned around and gasped in surprise. A brilliant smile spread across her face as she yelled, "Andy!" before bolting across the room toward her stepsister. The two immediately embraced each other and tears of joy fell down their faces.

"Oh my gosh! I have missed you so much!" Andy shrieked with excitement as she hugged the younger woman tightly to her chest. Pulling back slightly, she kissed Piper on the cheek before she looked over her body. "You doing okay, babe? I mean, you look good. It's just so nice to see you in person, finally. This is the first time since you turned eighteen that we have been away from each other this long."

Grabbing her stepsister's hand, the blonde led her toward the couch. As they sat, she smiled. "Yeah, I know. I can't believe you came. How did you get here?"

"Nikolai," Andy replied, holding on to Piper's hand. "We have talked a handful of times over the past couple days, actually. He told me about Paul and Grecoff arriving today and wanted me tucked away safely with you. He seems genuine and sincere or at least has when we've talked on the phone. How has he treated you P? I know he was able to help you acquire the money, but has he treated you well?"

Suddenly feeling ashamed and very overwhelmed, Piper stood up and began to pace the space in front of the couch. She had told her sister everything that was happening except having sex with Nikolai and their burgeoning relationship. Pausing a moment to look at Andy, she blurted, "I slept with him!"

"What?" Andy asked, looking at her sister in confusion.

"I slept with him!"

"Who?"

"Nikolai."

"What?" Andy shouted, completely taken off guard by the blonde's admission. "When?"

With a loud sigh, Piper said in one breath, "We've actually slept together several times, but the first time was my second night here. He ordered us some room service and then got me Oreos. Oreos, Andy! You know how I feel about those cookies. It just felt natural and—"

"P, slow down." The older woman smiled, shooting out her hand to cover Piper's mouth as she pulled her back on the couch. "Let's take it from the top. You said you have had sex with him several times, right? Start with the first time. What happened, exactly? I doubt you had sex with him because he had Oreos."

With another exasperated sigh, the blonde beauty leaned back on the sofa and began rubbing her arm. "Okay, so my first day here, I had isolated myself from him and tried to really figure out what in the hell was going on. That evening, I was looking for something to eat when Nikolai asked me if I wanted to join him for dinner. He ordered room service and we ended up talking about everything under the sun and laughing for hours. I mean, I was attracted to the guy from jump. I mean, you've seen him. He's gorgeous, Andy, but that's not all. He's funny, intelligent, compassionate. He's just an overall great guy."

"Uh huh... and how did Oreos and sex become a part of that?"

"I told him about my addiction to Oreos and he had never tried one, so he called and got me a package. I was showing him how to eat one and next thing I knew, we were having sex. And to top it off, I was the aggressor!"

"No freaking way!" Andy said in shock. Who the hell was this woman in front of her? "So, you've been sleeping with this guy the whole time you've been here? I can't believe you didn't tell me!"

"I'm so sorry I didn't tell you. I just didn't know what to do. Nik tried to tell me that sex would complicate things, initially, but I didn't listen. I just wanted him so bad, Andy, and that feeling has only grown. The sex has been mind-blowing but its's so much more than that. I'm afraid that I am falling in... never mind. After he takes care of Paul today, we will probably go our separate ways. I've enjoyed my time with him and will just have to live with the memories. I—"

Putting her hand up to Piper's mouth once again, Andy said, "Get out of your head, P, and take a deep breath. What were you going to say? Do you think you love him?"

"Yes," Piper replied softly. She was so overcome with emotion at finally admitting that out loud that she couldn't control the tears flowing down her face. "I don't know what in the hell has happened to me, but Nik is unlike any man I have ever met, and at this point, I can't picture my life without him. I can't explain it, but I trust him completely. I have even become his sexual submissive if you can believe that."

"Wait a minute," Andy replied, shaking her head in surprise. "His submissive? As in he is your dominant? Do you let him control you?"

"Yeah, but not like you're thinking. He's not like the guys we know in the world of BDSM. He isn't a dominant just to control women sexually or humiliate them. He's respectful and the couple times I used my safe word, he stopped immediately. Nik has earned my complete trust, something I have never given to a man before."

Andy sat there in stunned silence a moment after listening to the younger woman talk. "And you enjoy this? He's not mind controlling you or using sex as manipulation?"

Suddenly feeling very protective of her lover, she wiped vigorously at her tears and barked, "No, he's not mind controlling me or manipulating me sexually. Nik would never do that to a woman. He has made sure that I'm comfortable every step of the way and the sex is phenomenal. And the flogging… I've had an orgasm here and there with other men, but with Nik, it's multiple. I'm not going to give you the sex play by play, but I crave this man. It's like he has gotten in my blood."

"Who the hell are you and what did you do with my sister?

You have never let a man control you and now you're a sexual submissive to one? I think you may have lost your mind!"

"Really, Andy?" Piper said in a panicked voice, as she grew increasingly agitated. "You, of all people, are going to judge me? You are the one person I thought I could talk to about this. I—"

"I'm not judging you," the other woman interjected, grabbing her sister's face in her hands affectionately. "I'm just surprised by your actions, babe. This is not the Piper who left me five days ago. However, if you think you love this guy, then you take what belongs to you. Just know if he hurts you, I will be there to help beat his ass. If I'm being honest, I'm jealous as hell. I want a couple orgasms. Does he have any friends?"

"He might have a few." She chuckled, with a mixture of relief and anxiety. "I'm just so damn confused, sis. No, scratch that. I'm scared."

"You're only scared because you're overanalyzing this. How many times have we talked about that? You are your own worst enemy sometimes," Andy comforted gently, tucking her sister's platinum blonde hair behind one ear. "How do you think he feels about you? Have you told him that you love him?"

"No, I haven't. I chickened out at the last minute and told him I cared about him instead. He said the feeling was mutual, and I want to believe him, but the thought of him rejecting me is terrifying. I haven't exactly had the best luck with men in the past."

"Well, you said you trust him. If you do, then it's imperative you believe his words, too, in order to make a relationship work. Have you guys talked about being exclusive? I mean, if he's a dominant, I'm going to assume he has other submissives. Are you okay with him being intimate with other women?"

"Hell no!" Piper exclaimed emphatically. She wasn't about to share Nikolai with anyone. "We have talked about being exclusive, well, at least while he is here in the States. He said he was okay with that as long as I wanted him. He did ask me to go back to Russia with him when all of this is over."

"And what did you say?"

"I didn't say anything other than I would think about it." She agonized as a fresh set of tears threatened to fall. "Honestly, I don't know what to do."

"What does your gut say, P?" Andy asked, not adding that Nikolai had mentioned her moving to Russia with him and Piper. The comment had come completely out of the blue and she had not known how to respond so just didn't. She knew her sister had been acting odd the past few days but had never suspected that the younger woman was sleeping with the bratva leader. She had also noticed a softness to his tone when he talked about Piper so maybe her sister wasn't the only one with these insane feelings.

"It says go with him," she confessed with a light chuckle. "I mean, that's crazy, right? None of this makes any sense. I've known this guy for five days and my whole world has been turned completely upside down. I have suddenly become a millionaire, I quit med school, and now I think I have fallen in love. All of this is so far out of my comfort zone but, at the same time, it just feels right. I can't even begin to tell you how Nik makes me feel inside, but I like it. I feel like he makes me a better person."

"If that's how you feel, babe," Andy comforted, brushing the tears from her face, "then follow your heart. I know you're confused, but it sounds pretty simple to me."

"But Russia? I know you and I have talked about moving and starting our lives over, but that is a little extreme. Neither of us speak the language or know anything about the culture. How the hell do I get back into med school or you start your own vet practice? It's Russia, for crying out loud!"

"Well, it sounds as though Nikolai would make the perfect

guide in a transition like that. However, I'm not sure how you moving across the world became 'we'."

"If I'm moving out of the country, then so are you. There is no way I am leaving you behind. You're my only family and I need you, sis."

"Sweetheart, I love you too, but I don't think your man is going to want me living with you guys. I mean, you know me, I've always wanted to travel to Russia, but living there? Plus, there is still the little matter of the money. I know you gave me half of it and have already set up the account, but like I told you, I can't accept it. That money is yours and I need you to take it back. If you move, then I will too, but not with your money. It has to be on my own terms."

Shaking her head vigorously, Piper crossed her arms over her chest. "No, no, no! There is no way in hell I am taking the money back, Andy! I gave that to you as a gift. It's because of you that I am even alive today. You tried to protect me all those years ago from Maury, even when it meant putting yourself in harm's way. Even after I left foster care, you were there to help me pick up the pieces and get into med school. I could never repay you for loving me the way you did, so the least you could do is take the money. You don't have to struggle anymore, babe. It's my turn to take care of you for once. We are being given an opportunity to change our lives for the better and I say we take it."

Tears poured down Andy's face as she pulled Piper into her arms and crushed her in a loving embrace. The two held each other and cried as they allowed years of emotions to pour from their souls. The two little girls who had been brutalized were now women who controlled their own fates. No, they were not related by blood but had been connected to each other by some invisible force from the day they met. They allowed themselves to just feel for several minutes before Andy finally pulled back and chuckled awkwardly. Handing her sister a tissue as she dabbed at her own eyes, she half-smiled. "You cow! Only you can make me a blubbering mess. How did we go from Oreos and sex to crying?"

Piper laughed loudly as she, too, wiped at her own eyes. "What can I say? It's a gift!" She then embraced her sister once more before she threw her arm over her shoulder. "Okay, no more sappy talk. I hate crying and I know you do, too. You hungry?"

"Oh, my gawd! You and your stomach! Has Nikolai seen this dark side of you yet?"

"Yes, and guess what? He's a total foodie, too! He likes to eat just as much as I do. Another big plus for him, I might add. Let's go grab some grub."

"I was told we couldn't leave."

Rolling her eyes, Piper replied, "Yeah, I was too. Okay, room service it is."

"P?" Andy asked, gripping the younger woman's hand before she stood up. "Food isn't going to make this situation go away, babe, but I love you and I'm here for you if you need it."

With a loud sigh, Piper nodded at the older woman and squeezed her hand affectionately before she walked away to find the number for room service. She had no idea what she was going to do but she did know that she loved Nikolai. She just hoped the bratva leader loved her back.

Chapter 11

Piper sat on the floor against the cool glass as she watched the storm clouds blocking out the light from the full moon above. She reached under her black cropped hoodie to rub her stomach that was beginning to ache. The upset had started a couple hours ago and was building due to the emotional stress, anxiety, and fear she was feeling. It was almost 11:00 pm and she still had not heard from her lover or any of his men. Nikolai had been gone for almost twelve hours and she would assume that if everything were fine, he would have been home by now. What if something had happened and he was hurt? Or what if something had happened to his brother? Shaking herself mentally, she could not allow herself to think this way. Piper, however, was having a difficult time sitting in the suite doing nothing, especially if her giant Russian was hurt, or worse.

Jumping off the floor, she walked toward the bathroom where she quickly pulled her hair back in a loose bun. As she left the bathroom, she slid on her tennis shoes and headed back to the living room. She picked up her cellphone and contemplated calling Andy to ask her what she should do at this moment, but her sister had retired to her room a couple of hours ago. After the older woman had left, Piper had hopped in the shower and changed into a hoodie and matching leggings. She had tried watching television but that had done nothing to calm her nerves. Glancing toward the door of the suite again, Piper really didn't know what to do. She had promised Nikolai that she would stay in the room and wait for him to return, but what if he were in trouble and she could help him? Paul and Grecoff were Volkov enemies but this fiasco involved her. She would be damned if she allowed her lover to take the fall.

With a soft curse, she walked to the door of the suite and slowly opened it. Glancing outside, she saw two guards talking to each other in Russian. She watched one of them answer his cellphone before both hurriedly headed toward the private staff elevator. Piper took a deep breath before she ran to the main elevator and hopped in. When the doors closed, she glanced up and fought the tears that threatened to fall. She knew Nikolai was going to be pissed at her, but she just couldn't wait any longer for some type of confirmation that he was all right. She wasn't quite sure what she was going to do once she got to the main floor of the lobby, but she did have a loose plan. Hopefully, she didn't run into any of the guards, or if she did, maybe they would know some information regarding her lover.

As the elevator slowly descended, the feisty blonde became more and more anxious as it stopped and more people got on. Piper had spent the day thinking and talking to Andy about where she should take her relationship with Nikolai. Her heart and her head were at war with each other, and it had everything to do with the short length of time she had known him. What happened if she went to Russia and ended up getting stuck there? With her lover being in the bratva, would that limit where she could go and when? Would they be in constant danger? What if he got bored with her after a short time or took another submissive? Her heart screamed to simply push her fears aside and enjoy him, but her head was slamming on the brakes. What made things worse was the fact she had no idea where Nikolai stood or how he felt emotionally. There was no mistaking that he was attracted to her both physically and sexually, but those two things were a far cry from love or anything even resembling it. Piper was so conflicted and had never put herself in such a vulnerable position before. The feeling was so foreign that she wasn't quite sure how to handle it.

When the elevator finally reached the ground floor of the hotel, Piper stood back in the corner and allowed everyone else to exit first. As she began to step off, she was so engrossed in her own personal thoughts, she didn't see the solid mass of muscle standing before her. Running smack into his wide chest, she stumbled back and was grabbed by two strong arms. When she looked up to apologize, she was overcome with emotion as she immediately threw her arms around Nikolai's neck and hugged him tightly to her chest. The relief and feelings she felt were short lived, however, when he roughly pushed her back and gripped her arms. She watched his grey eyes darken to a charcoal color as he shielded his thoughts from her, and a scowl of anger covered his face.

"What the fuck are you doing out of the suite?" Nikolai snarled as he stared into her damp blue eyes. Fear leapt into his chest when he thought about her getting hurt, or worse, leaving him. With that last thought in mind, he asked, "Were you trying to leave me?"

"Leave you? No! I..." she said, confused, shaking her head. As she tried to embrace him, he again pushed her back into the corner of the elevator as the doors closed. Her eyes glanced from her Russian lover to Mikhas who stood by the elevator panel with his head down. "I was scared! I—"

"You were scared?" he retorted heatedly, pinning her in the corner as he towered over her. "Did you not tell me that you would trust me?"

"Yes, I did, but…" She trembled, wanting him to wrap her up in his arms but as she reached for him, Nikolai pushed her hands away.

"You were given direct orders to stay in the suite and wait for me, Piper! You promised me that you would stay there, yet you completely disobeyed me."

"Nik, I know I promised you, but I wanted to make sure—"

"Not another word from you until we reach the suite," he barked, the pulse beating wildly in his jaw, as tears sprang to her eyes.

"But you're not giving me a chance to explain," she pleaded, running her hand down his brawny arm, attempting to hold his hand. However, she let out a gasp when he ripped his hand from her grasp and turned around, giving her his back.

"You'll have plenty of time to explain after your punishment," he said in a soft, deadly tone just as Piper ran her hands up his back to his shoulders. Without turning to look at her, Nikolai said, "Take your hands off me, pet. I'm disappointed that you broke your promise. We will sort this out later."

Piper stood behind the bratva leader as the tears welled up in her eyes. Wiping away the wetness quickly, she exhaled shakily. She was torn between the joy of Nikolai being alive and safe and the anger she was feeling toward him for his sudden coldness. She knew she had broken her promise to him, but why wouldn't he just let her explain why she left the suite? She knew he would be upset, but his reaction was beyond anything she had expected. Willing the tears to stop, she crossed her arms over her chest and allowed the anger she was feeling to take over. He had mentioned a punishment. There was no way in hell she was going to let him touch her when he wouldn't even allow her to express her feelings.

"Everything okay, Niki?" Mikhas asked in Russian, as he glanced back at the blonde American. He had never seen his friend so angry.

"Not for you to worry about, Mik," he replied coolly without looking at the guard. "I can handle my woman, I assure you."

The seven-foot man said nothing as Nikolai watched him go back to looking at the elevator. Nik cracked his neck. He was livid! What in the hell was Piper thinking? Why had she been afraid? Had she really been trying to leave him? He had so many questions for her but was afraid to speak to her right now. Instead of talking or yelling, he wanted to beat her luscious ass and pound himself inside her first. When he was done making her submit once again, they could talk. What infuriated him most, was that his submissive had carelessly put herself in danger by coming down the elevator by herself. Although Piper didn't know it, Paul was dead but Grecoff had managed to escape. Nikolai had shot the bastard dead in the chest, but he had been wearing a bulletproof vest and managed to escape. Grecoff had fled with two of his men in a white van and now he and his brother had no idea where in the hell he had gone. The Volkovs had immediately made their way back to his suite and doubled the guards around the hotel but still no word of where Grecoff may be. They had men scouring the city for him but what if he had come back for Piper? What if his enemy had met her downstairs? A shiver ran through his body at that last thought. He knew exactly what would have happened and that terrified him to the core.

Reaching the penthouse suite, the elevator doors opened before Nikolai grabbed his submissive's arm and pushed her in front of him and Mikhas. Walking into the suite, his light grey eyes touched on his brother, Aleksandr, who was sitting on a plush, leather sofa nursing a bottle of vodka. He was seething with a quiet rage as his brother approached and asked in Russian, "Everything okay, Niki?"

"We need to talk privately," the younger man said between clenched teeth, as Piper jerked her arm out of his grip.

"Who's your friend?" Aleksandr asked curiously in English as the blonde's eyes shot to him.

"I know you are upset, my little lynx, but you'd better be nice to him. Your punishment is already severe enough," Nikolai whispered warningly in her ear before he allowed his hand to slide down her back to pat her bottom.

Gasping loudly and stiffening her posture, she looked at the handsome blond. Throwing her head back regally, she said, "My name is Piper Williamson, and I can assure you that Nikolai and I are not friends." Then as she stepped up to the older Volkov, she sharply asked, "Who the hell are you? Do you work for him like every other man around here does?"

"No, I don't. Nikolai works for me." The slightly taller Volkov smiled as she knitted her brow together in confusion. "I'm just kidding, sweetheart. I'm Nikolai's older, more attractive brother, Aleksandr. It's nice to finally meet you, Piper. Sorry we had to meet under circumstances such as these. I will admit that you are not what I was expecting."

"Don't expect anything from her, brother. This one belongs to me," Nikolai warned in Russian as he slid his arm protectively around her waist. Then to the voluptuous American, Nikolai said, "I need to talk to my brother, sweetheart. Wait in the bedroom for me, and I'll join you shortly. We can talk then about what occurred tonight."

Piper nodded her head before Nikolai kissed her softly on the neck. He knew she was internally seething and wanted to lash out at him but instead she walked away. When he heard the bedroom door close, Aleksandr gave him the bottle of vodka.

As he watched his younger brother down the clear liquid intently, Aleksandr inquired, "You looked like you could use a drink. Feeling a little tense this evening?"

"You don't know the half of it," Nikolai responded, taking another long swig of the vodka.

"Looks like Ms. Williamson is quite the handful," Aleksandr said, kicking back on the sofa and propping his feet up on the glass coffee table. "I take it the two of you don't get along very well?"

Nikolai didn't appreciate the smile he saw on his brother's face or the teasing nature of his tone. His mood was actually quite dark. "I'm not in the mood to talk about my interactions with Piper tonight, Zan. We have other problems."

"Such as?"

"One of our men saw Grecoff being picked up in a white van near the warehouse. We found a damaged bulletproof vest at the pickup spot. I guarantee it was his so that means the fucker isn't dead. Were you able to get any more information from Paul?"

"Morrison was insistent that the Chechens were behind the whole plan. Honestly, I'm not surprised. I made sure to record the confession so the council can see it. He also said that he and Grecoff had met with Piper a few weeks ago. Has she mentioned that to you?"

"She did. Piper told me she was approached by them one night and that they wanted to talk. She answered a few questions before Grecoff came on to her. She told him no and he hit her a couple of times, but she was able to get out of there without anything else happening. She also said Paul never mentioned anything about being her half-brother or the money. She only discovered that piece of information after we met."

"Do you believe her? What's her story?" Aleksandr asked, watching his brother's eyes as they kept averting to the hallway that led to the bedroom where Piper had gone.

"I do. Everything that she's told me so far has checked out," Nikolai responded before dropping down in the chair perpendicular to his brother. "She's a medical student who works part time in a club as a dancer. She's twenty-three and has had a pretty rough past based on what we've found. She hasn't confirmed a lot of the history because she's reluctant to talk about it."

Aleksandr rubbed his bearded chin as he listened to Nikolai speak. Sounded like he needed to investigate Ms. Williamson's past himself. His brother was clearly interested in the blonde beauty and there was no way in hell he would let anyone hurt Nikolai. "We know Paul is corrupt and has been for several years. Is Piper?"

"No," the younger Volkov replied emphatically, shaking his head before he took another drink. "If she's anything, it's too honest. She's quite the enigma, reminds me of Sophia to some degree. My little lynx is emotionally damaged like your American and won't allow herself to be happy."

"Tell me about it," Aleksandr scoffed, rolling his eyes before running an agitated hand through his dirty blond hair. Looking directly into eyes the same as his, he asked, "Have you slept with her? I want the truth, Niki."

It was moments like this that Nikolai hated his bond with his brother. Aleksandr had always been able to read him like an open book, without a word being spoken. Without batting an eye, he said, "Yes, I have. Several times, in fact, and I plan on doing it again. I'm going to bring her back to Russia with me until I can kill Grecoff. Do you have any problems with that?"

"Should I?"

"No."

"Good, because I got my own shit to worry about right now," Aleksandr countered, taking the bottle of vodka from his brother and taking another drink. "You know the council is pushing for me to take over. If I do it, I want you right there beside me. How would you feel about that?"

"You know I would have no problems with it, Zan, so why don't you tell me what is really on your mind?" Nikolai replied worriedly as he watched his brother gaze out the window that made up one wall. Outside, the Vegas lights twinkled below them. "You've been in a shitty mood since your plane landed. Plus, don't think I haven't noticed that Vor isn't here. I'm assuming something has happened between you and Sophia. Care to talk about it?"

"Yeah, I do," Aleksandr sighed, keeping his eyes on the city lights outside. The senior bratva leader really didn't want to involve his younger brother in his relationship problems when he was clearly having issues of his own.

"Come on, Zan. I know you see me as your little brother, but I'm a grown man. I also happen to like Sophia," the dark-haired man responded, thinking of the attorney who was Aleksandr's new love interest. "We've dealt with shit like Morrison and Chechen our whole fucking lives and you've never showed emotion like this. That only leaves one person as the source of your foul mood."

Finally looking at Nikolai, Aleksandr's voice was soft and full of emotion as he said, "I fucked things up with Sophia and I don't know how to fix it."

"I doubt that. What happened?" the younger Volkov asked. He had never in his life seen his older brother emotional over anything, let alone a woman.

"Sophia thinks I lied to her," Aleksandr scoffed, running an agitated hand through his hair as he removed his feet from the coffee table and leaned forward by placing his elbows on his knees. "She's out of her fucking mind because I've never lied to anyone in my life! So, I didn't tell her about the attempts on her life while she was in my home. That's not me lying about it. I just didn't tell her. I wanted her to feel safe in my home. I wanted her to enjoy being there with me. I wanted... I wanted her to fall in love with me, Nik."

Reaching out, Nikolai affectionately rubbed his brother's broad shoulder. "I think she has, Zan. You don't know this, but when I met Sophia, I was hoping to share her with you and made the mistake of expressing that. She let me know quickly that she belonged to you, and you alone. I see the way she looks at you. She loves you, too, she's just scared to admit it. Given her past, I can understand why." After a long moment of silence from his brother, he asked, "Are you willing to fight for Sophia, Zan? If you are, then go get your damn woman, but if you're not, let her go. Sophia is a risk worth taking and I've never known you to walk away from a challenge."

Before Aleksandr could respond to his brother, Mikhas walked into the room and looked directly at the elder Volkov. "I'm sorry to interrupt, boss, but the pilot called and the plane is ready."

"Thank you, Mikhas. Call Petya and have him meet me downstairs with the car in five." When his second in command walked away, Aleksandr stood and grabbed his jacket off the back of the nearby chair. Looking at Nikolai, a smile touched his face. "Thanks for the pep talk, Niki, and by the way, Sophia *is* worth it. Will I see you back in Russia soon?"

Nikolai stood as well and pulled his brother in for a tight, loving embrace. Pulling back, he grabbed Aleksandr by the nape of his neck. "Da. Give me a day or two to finish up here and I'll be home. Go easy on Sophia, okay? It will all work out in the end."

"Of course, it will. I'm one hell of a catch." Aleksandr smiled before he patted Nikolai's face lovingly and headed toward the door.

Watching the door close behind his brother, the younger bratva leader's thoughts immediately turned to his blonde submissive. Sitting back down in the chair, he took off his shoes and socks before removing his suit jacket. As he did this, he thought about the words he had just said to Zan regarding Sophia. Piper and the redhead were similar in some respects. Both had grown up alone and had been treated like sex objects by men. They both had also made it to their current stations in life through their own will, hard work, and determination. Nikolai had been raised in a completely different environment than his woman and had at no time ever been alone. Where Piper trusted no one and had been betrayed multiple times, he had always had someone to confide in and did not really know the sting of betrayal personally. Maybe he should heed his own advice to his brother and go easy on his woman. He not only wanted her as his full time submissive, but he wanted her in his life always. Nikolai Volkov had finally found a woman he could spend the rest of his life with, someone he... loved. With a loud sigh, he stood up and made his way down the hall toward the bedroom. He was tired of denying his feelings for Piper and needed to know if she felt the same. His head found it ridiculous that he could love a woman after only five days, but his heart screamed otherwise. Everything about her was unique. His body literally came to life when she was near and that had never happened with any other woman. He knew she was different the night he met her, but her fate had been sealed the first night she completely submitted to him.

Heading into the bedroom, he was not surprised to find her sitting in the middle of the bed with her head buried in her hands. He could tell she was quietly sobbing, and he immediately felt remorse and guilt for being so harsh with her in the elevator. Walking over to the bed, he sat down on the edge and placed one hand on her knee. Her sad blue eyes immediately met his as she wiped at the moisture on her flaw-less face. He then leaned in to place a kiss on her full lips, but she turned her head and wouldn't allow it. With a heavy sigh, he said, "We need to talk, Piper."

"Oh?" she asked, her voice laced with venom. "You're going to let me talk now? How very noble of you. Why, just a few minutes ago, I had to keep my mouth shut and obey your command. You can shove your orders up your ass! I'm done taking those from you, Nikolai."

"I probably deserve some of that vitriol I hear in your tone," he confessed, searching her eyes.

"You think?" she scoffed, crossing her arms over her chest. "You hurt my feelings."

"I know I did," Nikolai agreed gently as his arms shot out and pulled her struggling frame across his lap to straddle. As she writhed and tried to break his grip, he apologized, "And I'm sorry, love. I thought... I thought you might get hurt or that you might leave me. I don't think I could recover from either."

Piper instantly stopped struggling as his hands slid under her top to rub the bare skin of her back. Cupping his hand-some face in her hands, she saw an odd vulnerability in the depths of his eyes. Rubbing her nose against his, she said, "I had no intention of getting hurt and I definitely wasn't leaving you, baby. I was scared that I would never see you again or that something had happened to you and that's something I couldn't recover from. In my defense, I had not heard from you all day and after Andy went to bed, all I had were my thoughts, which is not a good thing. I didn't even really have a plan when I got in the elevator other than asking hotel staff if they had seen you. I know I broke my promise to you, Nik, and I'm sorry for that, but I won't apologize for loving you."

"What did you say?" he asked, gripping her shoulders and

pushing her back slightly. Had he just heard her correctly? Did Piper love him?

Taking a deep breath, she pushed herself off his lap and stood up. She hated the tears that sprang to her eyes and the sudden feeling of fear she felt. Hugging herself tightly, she began to pace the space in front of him. "I said I love you, Nikolai!" she blurted before she ranted. "I know you probably think I'm crazy for saying that and I don't know where and when it happened, but it did. I don't expect you to feel the same way, but I have given your earlier proposal a lot of thought. I want to go to Russia with you if the offer still stands. I mean, I'll be your submissive, but I can't watch you with other women. If you plan on having multiple partners, then I might as well just stay here in the States. I—"

Nikolai cut off her ramblings by abruptly turning her around and passionately capturing her mouth with his. His hands molded her plump bottom as he caressed her tongue with his. When he began to feel her hands slide into his hair and her body melting into his, he broke the kiss and rubbed his nose against her neck. There he huskily whispered with a smile on his face, "I love you, too, Piper, and just so you know, you are the only woman I want, now or ever."

"Really?" she asked, her smile blinding as it exposed straight, white teeth. "You love me? Do you really mean that?"

"Have I ever lied to you?" he questioned, loving the brilliant smile on her face and the small gap between her two front teeth. "Like you, I don't know when or how it happened, but I wanted you the moment we met. Hell, if I'm being honest, I have wanted you since I first saw your picture."

She smashed her mouth to his for a quick kiss before she pushed back and said excitedly, "I was so worried that you wouldn't reciprocate my feelings, Nik. That first night we met in my condo, I wanted you so bad but thought maybe I was going crazy because I had never felt that way before. So, what do we do now, baby? How do we make this work? I mean, if I'm going with you back to Russia, there is so much that we need to talk about and plan."

"We will have plenty of time to plan our future." He chuckled before he slid his hands under her cropped hoodie and jerked the shirt over her head. He nuzzled her long, slender neck as he unclipped her bra and it fell to the floor. Massaging the large, tanned globes, he huskily said, "Right now, I am going to make love to my submissive."

Piper's fingers quickly unbuttoned his linen shirt as his mouth devoured her neck and shoulders. She placed kisses across his chest before her warm tongue lapped at his male nipples, then pushed him back to sit on the side of the bed as she began removing her underwear and pants slowly while his grey eyes watched her hungrily. When her clothes were off, she knelt before him on the floor and lowered her head. In a soft, sultry voice she purred, "I'm yours for the taking, master."

"Is that so?" he asked as he stood up and circled her, unbuckling his pants. Nikolai then pulled out his semi-hard cock and began stroking it with long, slow movements as a sexy grin played on his lips. "Mmm, what should I do with you first, my little lynx?"

Her head lifted leisurely, and her own eyes were darkened with lust and passion as they connected with his. Her voice was erotic and sensual when she replied, "Anything you like, sir. Would you like me to suck that delicious cock you're holding?"

The sound that escaped Nikolai's throat was gruff and primal as he slid his hand into the back of her hair and jerked her up on her knees in front of him. He rubbed his organ lovingly across her lips and cheeks before her tongue shot out and traced the tip of it. His head fell back when her hands replaced his and she sucked the head into her mouth. His stomach muscles twitched, and he gritted his teeth as one free hand massaged his balls and she deepthroated the length of him in her sweet mouth. She continued the brutal massage as she dropped his cock with a pop and nibbled on the veiny underside. Then to his satisfaction and delight, Piper again put his dick between her lips and began sucking it with fast, short strokes. It didn't take long for the pressure in his balls to build.

"Let me come in your mouth, sweetheart," he ordered breathlessly, his hands pulling at her curly hair as he assisted her movements. She responded to his command by sucking just on the head as she stroked him with both hands. His breathing became ragged moments before he shot in her hot mouth. He grunted and groaned loudly, and his body convulsed painfully as she sucked the sweet, salty liquid down her throat. He dribbled his essence down on her plump breasts as he pulled his cock from her grip and jerked her up roughly. He then crushed his mouth to hers in a fiery kiss as he lifted her off the ground. Just as her body began to melt into his, he tossed her on top of the bed. His eyes dared her to move as he barked, "You stay right there."

Piper chewed on her bottom lip as she watched him disappear out of the room a moment before he came back in with a handful of items. Seeing the restraints, vibrating wand, and flogger made her pussy begin to ache painfully between her legs. Her hand slid down her body to circle the sensitive nub. Just as she began to pick up a rhythm, Nikolai grabbed her leg and dragged her to the edge of the bed. She cried out in a mixture of pain and pleasure when his hand came down painfully on her neatly trimmed mound.

"Did I give you permission to please yourself, pet?"

"N-no, sir," she panted anxiously in response. "Wh-what are you going to do with me, master?"

"Well, before I fuck you into submission," Nikolai replied, hungrily licking his lips before he bent over her and ran his tongue seductively along her mouth. "There is the little matter of you disobeying my orders to stay in the suite. Now drop your hands down by your side."

The blue-eyed American obeyed her dominant's orders and her wrists were quickly shackled to her ankles. She lay bare and exposed before him with her legs wide open and her pussy dripping wet. Her eyes widened with nervousness as she watched him strip off his pants and underwear and stand before her in all his glorious nakedness. Her core visibly pulsed as he picked up a black leather flogger and ran the tresses down his bare chest and abdomen before he allowed them to flow over his hardening cock. Looking up into his eyes, she said in a barely audible whisper, "I love you, master."

"I love you, too," he sincerely responded, looking deep into her eyes as a handsome smile crossed his face. Just as he did this, his fingers slid in and out of her vaginal entrance before he hungrily tasted her essence. A shiver ran through him as her sweet taste played on his tongue just as she whimpered and ground her hips uncomfortably. Before she could say another word, Nikolai allowed the flogger to strike her breasts and abdomen. He watched in complete satisfaction as she began begging him for more and her pussy drenched the bedding.

Piper cried out, on the edge of an intense orgasm, as her lover lightly struck her repeatedly while she fought against the restraints. Hearing a low frequency buzzing begin, her head shot off the bed just as her eyes settled on the pink, vibrating wand her lover was holding. When he struck her again with the flogger and put the toy to her clitoris, she screamed out his name as she came hard and fast. Her body writhed in glorious agony uncontrollably as the vibrations of the wand were kicked up and the second orgasm tore through her sensitive frame. As she floated in the clouds with euphoria, Nikolai scooped her up under her hips seconds before his mouth captured the sensitive nub between her legs. As her pussy pulsed and her release flowed from between her legs, her Russian lover licked up every drop of the sweetness. She rode the wave of ecstasy before he dropped her back on the bed and quickly removed her restraints. He then wrapped her up in his muscular arms as he eased his cock balls deep inside her and captured her mouth in a steamy, wet kiss.

Piper held on to her lover tightly and sucked on his neck as he pounded himself deep inside her core. When her fingers plucked at his male nipples, he grabbed her hands and locked them above her head.

"Just for that, sweetheart, you are going to make love to me," Nikolai growled, his teeth nibbling on her slender neck. He then abruptly rolled them over with his cock still deep in her warm, wet core so she could straddle his lap. To his surprise, she began to move off him. He grabbed her hips and asked, "And just where do you think you're going?"

Leaning over him, she ran her tongue over his lips. "I'm not going far, sir." Piper smiled before kissing his lips. "You are going to like this, I promise."

The muscular giant then kissed her once more and released her hips. She pushed Nikolai's legs together and straddled his lap again. Facing his feet, she reached under herself with one hand, to guide his massive cock back into her pussy before she sat back on it and moaned. She massaged her own breasts as she began to bounce up and down his length slowly. She then gripped his lower legs and allowed him to watch her pink, wet cunt sliding all the way up him, only to slide back down. She cried out in pain as he smacked her butt cheeks with both hands before he gripped her waist and helped her ride him at a frantic pace. She bounced up and down on him and inched closer and closer to another release. Just when she gripped his thighs and her nails dug into his tanned skin, the yell of intense pleasure punched through her chest and bounced off the walls. Her vaginal walls clenched around his cock before Nikolai shot his load deep into her womb. She felt him sit up and his arms hug her tightly to his chest as he kissed and nibbled at her shoulder while he rode his own intense wave. To prolong his pleasure, she contracted her muscles and kissed the pulsing vein in his neck as her hand played with his black hair.

A girlish giggle escaped her lips when he pushed her off his lap and rolled her back under him again. The smile of satisfaction on his own lips had her chuckling. "Someone looks like he enjoyed himself."

"I might have... a little." He laughed as she lightly punched his chest. He then lazily gazed into her eyes as he asked, "Now before your punishment, I do believe you were saying something about moving to Russia."

"Yes, I was," Piper replied awkwardly as she massaged his shoulders. "I didn't know if I was going to live in my own place or with you. I mean, will I even be able to get into a med school there and finish my residency?"

"You leave all that to me," Nikolai said, kissing her lips again. "Some of the best doctors in the world are friends of mine. With your grades, I have no doubt we can get you in a program. As for where you will live, it will be with me, in my home."

"Are you sure, baby? I mean, we haven't known each other long and I don't want you to feel obligated to—"

The Russian silenced her with another kiss before he said seriously, "I don't feel obligated. I love you. I know we don't know everything about each other yet but living together will give us an opportunity to get to know each other better. Just so you know, my little lynx, I want to know everything there is to know about you."

"Same here." She grinned, tracing his masculine jaw with her nail. "Are you going to be okay with Andy, too?"

"Da. I anticipated that and will make sure to help her acclimate to our culture. Andy will be in good hands, I promise."

With a sigh, a thin veil of uncertainty came over her eyes as she fretted. "Look, can I be honest with you? Your lifestyle scares the hell out of me. I mean, will you be in constant danger? Do I have to worry about you coming home to me every day?"

"Nyet," Nikolai responded, shaking his head. "I don't live my life in fear, pet, and neither will you. I don't expect you to really understand it until you are submerged in it. There are guards around us 24/7 who see to our safety, and those same men will be with you and Andy. However, you will be free to come and go from our home, provided security is by your side. You're not going to be my prisoner, sweetheart. You are going to be my woman, submissive, partner... whatever label you want to give us."

"So, you have no problems with being in an exclusive relationship?"

"I was taken off the market the day I met you, love." He rolled her on top of him again as he lay back against the pillows.

"So, what next? I'm assuming with Paul and Grecoff dead, we will be leaving the States soon."

"Paul is dead, but Grecoff is not," he confessed as she looked at him with confusion. "However, before you begin asking questions, he was wearing a bulletproof vest and managed to get away. This does not impact you or your safety in any way, though, and we already have men working on finding him. Until we kill him, though, you and Andy both will have added protection. I don't think he will try to contact either of you because his issues are not with you, but with Zan and me."

"Are you worried that he'll come after you and your brother? You will have added security, too, right?"

"Of course, love, but honestly? I'm not worried about Grecoff, and neither should you be. His father and Paul are both dead and he has nowhere to run. After we present the meeting from today to the council, there is not a man alive who would even think about helping him." When he saw her brow knit together in thought, Nikolai leaned forward and kissed her. "You think too much, pet. You trust me, da?"

"Absolutely."

"Then stop fretting and get out of your head," the Russian chastised, feeling the damp curls from her pussy rubbing against the solid muscles of his stomach. "I've got you, Piper. No one will ever hurt you again."

A smile touched her lips before she bent her head down and kissed the skin directly above his heart. When her eyes met his again, there was a vulnerability there. "You promise? I want you to always be honest with me, even if you think I can't handle it."

He caressed her face lovingly with his thumb. "I will always be honest with you as long as you promise to always love me." Nikolai then rolled her back under him once again before he slid his cock into her core. Nuzzling her neck, he whispered, "Will you always love me, Piper?"

"Always, Nik," she replied, cupping his face with her hands and capturing his mouth for a kiss. When she pulled back, a brilliant smile touched her lovely face as she sighed. "You're stuck with me, master. You'd better get used to this face."

"Good, because I happen to love your face." He grinned back, easing himself out of her pussy only to push himself back in. "Now, this dominant wants to make love to his submissive. Any objections?"

"None," she whispered before her lover silenced her with another passionate kiss.

Epilogue

Piper pulled her coat closer to her body as the cold, Russian air sliced through her when she exited the black Escalade. She was immediately flanked on her left by Mikhas, who walked with her to the door of the modern, two-story mansion. Once the door closed and the two were inside, the guard left her as she took off her coat and handed it to the servant who immediately appeared.

"Hey, Yuna." The blonde smiled, taking off her hat and gloves also. "Is Nikolai home yet?"

"Nyet," the older woman replied as she hung up Piper's coat. "Should be home soon, though, mistress. There are some plyushka and black tea in the study."

"Yuna, thank you so much. A girl could really get used to such good treatment." She chuckled, placing her hand on the woman's shoulder. "If you need anything, you know where to find me."

Heading toward the study, Piper could not get over how different her life had been in the last three weeks. The morning after Paul had been murdered, she and Nikolai had enjoyed breakfast with Andy and discussed the big transition to Russia. Since arriving in the foreign land, she and her new dominant lover had become even closer, and she couldn't be happier. He had been instrumental in helping her navigate the culture and had already gotten her connected with a doctor who headed the medical residency program. She had just returned from a meeting with him and would be starting the program in a couple of weeks. She was amazed at how well she was assimilating to the country and its people and just how comfortable she felt. Nikolai had introduced her to several people and made sure to let them know that she was "his woman". Her days consisted of crash courses in Russian culture and language and her nights were spent having the most amazing sex of her life. Piper had even been able to spend time with Nikolai's brother, Aleksandr, and his fiancée, Sophia. The couples had enjoyed a handful of nights together and both were very kind to her. Sophia had quickly become one of her good friends and she liked the sharp-tongued, feisty attorney. Today, was particularly exciting, because Andy's plane would be arriving in Moscow tonight and she couldn't wait to see her again. Her stepsister had stayed behind in Vegas to sum up their affairs in the States. Life couldn't be better for her and Piper had finally found the peace she had been looking for.

As soon as she stepped into the study, she went for the pastry sitting on the table. The plyushka were so good but still not an Oreo cookie. Picking up the treat, she took a bite of it before she walked over to the desk and sat. Reaching into the bag she was carrying, she took out the paperwork the head of the medical program had given her and started working on it. She worked for several minutes, when, suddenly, she heard the door to the study open. A beautiful smile touched her lips when she saw Nikolai sauntering across the room with a colorful bouquet of flowers.

"Why, Mr. Volkov," she began as she stood to walk around

the desk and into his arms. "I would have never pegged you as a floral man."

"Well, it's the strangest thing, really," he said, setting the flowers on the desk and wrapping his arms around her, "it wasn't until I went to America and found the woman of my dreams that I even thought about flowers. She forever changed me, though."

Piper giggled before she captured his mouth in a loving kiss. When she broke the kiss, she fingered his strong jaw. "They're gorgeous, babe. I can't thank you enough for the bouquet."

"Oh, I can think of several ways you can thank me," Nikolai responded huskily as he nuzzled her neck and his hands ran down her back to massage her bottom.

"Later, Romeo." The platinum blonde laughed, hugging him to her chest once more. "Right now, I have to finish this application. It's due tomorrow."

"Is this for the medical program? How did your meeting with Micha go?"

"Amazing! I was able to review Micha's medical credentials and he is a remarkable doctor on paper. He was even nicer in person. I think working with him will be a perfect fit."

"I'm glad to hear that." He smiled, patting her bottom once again before he sat down in a chair and pulled her on his lap. "I know we had talked about meeting Andy tonight for dinner but Krugan called and said there was a weather delay that interfered with takeoff, so she won't be here until early tomorrow morning."

"Oh well, that's okay. I can always spend time with her tomorrow. She'll probably sleep most of the day anyway."

"Well then, since our plans have suddenly changed, I thought we could have dinner with Zan and Sophia before we go with them to Club Carnage."

"Club Carnage? Is that the BDSM club you've been talking about?"

"Da," Nikolai replied sensually as he pulled at her ear with his teeth. "There are all types of naughty things we can do there."

"Is that so?" Piper smiled playfully, loving how affectionate her man was. "And you're assuming that I will just let you have your way with me? I might change my mind, or I just may not be in the mood."

"Well, then, I'll have to make sure I have my Oreos with me if you need some persuasion." The Russian grinned as the blonde burst out in laughter and hugged him tightly.

"It's not fair that you know my weaknesses, Nik, especially since I haven't learned yours yet, but I still love you anyway."

"*You* are my weakness, my little lynx," he said gently, kissing her lips softly. "Now say it again."

Piper felt the moisture flooding her eyes as her hands played with his hair. Never in her life, had she felt more loved than she did right now. Nikolai made her feel feminine, soft, and adored. She wasn't sure what she had done in her life to deserve him, but she would do everything in her power to keep him.

"I love you, Mr. Volkov. More than you will ever know."

"I love you, too," he said huskily before he picked her up and sat her on the desk. He then reached for the bottom of her shirt and jerked it over her head. Capturing her lips in a fiery passionate kiss, he moaned, "Now show me how much you need me."

"Yes, master," Piper groaned, pulling at his bottom lip with her teeth. She would be glad to show him how much she needed him for the rest of her life.

Jessie Jones

My name is Jessie Jones and I am a 43-year-old woman who is a new author with Blushing Books Publications. My debut novel, "The Taking," is the first installment of the "Finding Forever" series. I have been telling stories since I was old enough to talk, however, didn't begin writing them down until I was about 7 years old. I am currently not married, and I live in the Middle of Nowhere Indiana with my sister, nephew, and 5 rescue babies (all dogs). When I am not writing steamy, erotic romances you will find me traveling, ghost hunting, watching scary movies, playing with the four-legged babies, and listening to Panic at the Disco.

You can connect with me on Facebook at https://www.facebook.com/profile.php?id=100045892626808 or at Twitter at https://twitter.com/JessieJBooks . You can also email me directly at jessiejonesromance2019@gmail.com

Don't miss these exciting titles by Jessie Jones and Blushing Books!

Finding Forever Series
The Taking
The Seduction
The Falling
The Coming Storm
The Road to Redemption
Endless Love

Finding Forever Collection

His Reluctant Submissive Series
Aleksandr
Nikolai

Blushing Books

Blushing Books is the oldest eBook publisher on the web. We've been running websites that publish steamy romance and crotica since 1999, and we have been selling eBooks since 2003. We have free and promotional offerings that change weekly, so please do visit us at http://www.blushingbooks.com/free.

Blushing Books Newsletter

Please join the Blushing Books newsletter
to receive updates & special promotional offers.
You can also join by using your mobile phone:
Just text BLUSHING to 22828.

Every month, one new sign up via text messaging will receive
a $25.00 Amazon gift card, so sign up today!